Wild THING
GOES CAMPING!

Look out for

and

Wild THING GETS A DOG!

Wild THING
GOES CAMPING!

Emma Barnes

Illustrated by Jamie Littler

■SCHOLASTIC

First published in the UK in 2015 by Scholastic Children's Books
An imprint of Scholastic Ltd
Euston House, 24 Eversholt Street,
London, NW1 1DB, UK
Registered office: Westfield Road, Southam, Warwickshire, CV47 0RA
SCHOLASTIC and associated logos are trademarks and/or registered
trademarks of Scholastic Inc.

Text copyright © Emma Barnes, 2015
Illustration copyright © Jamie Littler, 2015

The rights of Emma Barnes and Jamie Littler to be identified as the author
and illustrator of this work have been asserted by them.

ISBN 978 1407 13797 1

Cover illustration © Jamie Littler, 2015

A CIP catalogue record for this book is
available from the British Library.

Printed and bound by CPI Group (UK) Ltd, Croydon, CR0 4YY
Papers used by Scholastic Children's Books are made
from wood grown in sustainable forests.

1 3 5 7 9 10 8 6 4 2

This is a work of fiction. Names, characters, places,
incidents and dialogues are products of the author's imagination
or are used fictitiously. Any resemblance to actual people,
living or dead, events or locales is entirely coincidental.

www.scholastic.co.uk

For Abby

1

"You do it!"

"No, you do it!"

"It's your turn!"

"No, it isn't!"

"Well, I'm not doing it! And that's final!"

Dad and Gran glared at each other. I couldn't help giggling.

They both turned on me. "It's all very well you laughing, but this is serious!" said Gran.

"Yes, Kate, you're only laughing because you don't have to get involved," Dad said, waggling a sock at me. (He was sorting laundry into baskets on the floor.)

At that moment the cause of all the trouble, my little sister Wild Thing, came skipping into the kitchen. Her real name is Josephine, but I always call her Wild Thing. She's five years old, and she's *awful*.

Today she was wearing a cowboy hat and singing loudly as (for some reason known only to herself) she waved a lasso around her head.

She didn't seem at all concerned about being the cause of a family crisis. But then, she's used to it.

"You don't really want to go to Clementine's birthday party, do you?" said Dad hopefully to Wild Thing. I glanced at the invitation lying on front of me on the kitchen table. Dad had discovered it in Wild Thing's bag when Gran brought us back from school.

To Josephine
☆ Please come to Clementine's
5th Birthday Party
Games, treasure hunt and
☆ fun! ☆

The problem was, Wild Thing is too young to stay at birthday parties by herself, and both Dad and Gran were desperate not to be the one to take her!

Wild Thing said, "Do so want to go! Want birthday cake." And she disappeared into the hall.

Dad groaned. Then he said, "I don't understand why they've even invited her. When she was at nursery she never got invited to birthday parties!"

"Not after that time she sat on Ellie's birthday cake," I agreed.

"Or the time she took all the birthday boy's presents under the table," Gran added. "And wouldn't give them back."

Dad and Gran looked at each other. Their mouths drooped as they remembered previous parties.

"Cheer up," I said. "Maybe she'll be so awful at this party she won't be invited to any ever again."

Dad and Gran did not look like they found this comforting. Dad went back to sorting socks. "Why don't we say she's sick?" he suggested.

"No!" shouted Wild Thing, reappearing. "Not sick! Want cake!"

She went bounding out through the back hall that leads to the garden. Our pet, Hound Dog, followed her.

"Oh well, we can just think about it later," said Gran, pushing the invitation aside. She turned to me. "I've got some very exciting news, Kate."

"What's that?"

"My good friend Julia – you remember Julia, don't you?"

"I think so."

"Well, her granddaughter, Fiona, is starting at your school this week. And she's going to be in your class!"

I could tell I was supposed to be overjoyed at this news. But somehow all I could manage was a rather flat "Oh."

"Such a lovely girl," Gran went on enthusiastically. "So talented! So smart! So polite! And always does so well at school!"

I don't know why it is, but somehow whenever grown-ups rave on about other children, I always find myself taking against them.

"She'd make a lovely best friend for you, Kate," Gran said.

"But I've already got a best friend." I wasn't about to swap Bonnie for *anyone*.

Wild Thing skipped by again. She seemed to be covered in soil now, but I didn't draw attention to this. "Lovely jubbly, lovely jubbly!" she chorused before disappearing towards the stairs.

"Now I don't want you to take against poor Fiona," Gran went on. "I remember when your dad was growing up, I tried to encourage him to be friends with that lovely boy Nigel—"

"We had nothing in common," said Dad.

"He was delightful!" Gran insisted. "Always so clean! Such beautiful manners. And he's turned out terribly well. He has his own accountancy firm." My dad is a rock guitarist. (Or at least, he's a rock guitarist some of the time. But now he's part retired so he can look after Wild Thing and me. There's a lot for him to do, because Mum died when Wild Thing was only little.)

"Just because *you* thought he was marvellous," said Dad, who was struggling with a duvet cover, "doesn't mean he was the perfect friend for me, and this Fiona might not be the perfect friend for Kate, either."

I gave Dad a grateful smile. I'm not sure he noticed – the duvet cover was winning the struggle at that moment.

"No," Gran retorted, "but it's very hard starting a new school, and I'm sure that Fiona could do with a friendly face."

She was right, of course. Suddenly I felt a bit bad. "All right," I promised. "I'll be specially friendly."

"Good girl, Kate! I knew I could rely on you."

I sighed. Sometimes I get fed up with being the one everyone relies on. I mean, nobody ever expects Wild Thing to be helpful. But maybe they should. . .

"What about Wild Thing?" I asked, as my little sister came skipping into the room again. "Does Fiona have a little sister?"

7

"Yes, actually she does." Gran sounded a lot more cautious.

"So?"

"I'm not sure they'd have that much in common."

Wild Thing skidded to a halt.

"What's her name?" she asked. "Will she be in my class?"

"I think she might be," Gran admitted. "She's called Nerisa. She's a lovely girl. She always knows how to behave." (Wild Thing never knows how to behave!)

"Maybe she can be in my gang," said Wild Thing. "Does she like mud?"

"I don't think she does like mud, no. Actually, Nerisa is always very clean and tidy."

"How about digging?"

"No, I'm sure she doesn't like digging."

"Worms?"

"Worms! Certainly not! Nerisa is a very gentle girl, who loves ballet and kittens and making things out of silver paper."

"Well, she can't be in my gang then!" said Wild Thing, and she stomped off towards the garden. As she went past the laundry basket, she grabbed one of the clean sheets. Dad, who was now sorting the dirty clothes, didn't notice.

"Wild Thing," I shouted after her, "what do you think you're—"

"Kate," Gran interrupted me. "Just leave your little sister be. She's only trying to help."

I stared at her in amazement. But before I could say anything, Dad gave a huge yell. He jumped up, throwing a pair of Wild Thing's jeans away from him. As they flew across the room, a shower of pink, wriggly things came down on us, like a pink, wriggly hailstorm.

2

"Eek!" I screeched as one of them bounced off my head.

"What's going on?" Gran asked, leaping up.

I held out one of the pink, wriggly things. "Worms! It's raining worms!"

"Just wait till I get hold of your sister," Dad growled.

"But what – why—?"

"I was just emptying Wild Thing's pockets, ready for the wash, and I put my hand in and felt all these . . . these smooth things squirming about." He shuddered. "It gave me a bit of a shock. I should have realized she'd just been collecting worms from the garden. Again." He sighed.

"That girl needs sorting out!" said Gran

sternly. "But meanwhile, I've got to go home and put on my tea, or I'll be late for Zumba. Now, where's my handbag. . ." Gran reached under her chair. "That's funny," she said, frowning.

"Maybe it's in the hall," said Dad, who was helping me gather up worms.

It wasn't.

"I hope I didn't leave it behind at the supermarket earlier," said Gran worriedly.

"No," I said, picking a worm out of Gran's coffee cup. "It was definitely here. I remember you opened it to give Wild Thing and me a mint earlier."

We all looked at one another. Then: "Wild Thing!" Dad shouted. "Come here!"

There was a pause. Dad shouted, "Wild Thing!" again. Finally, a distant voice called, "I'm busy!"

It came from the direction of the garden.

We all set out to investigate.

Our garden is not the tidiest I've ever seen.

It's not even the second tidiest. There's a rather weedy patch of grass near the house, then there's the bit where Dad has recently started to dig out a vegetable patch, and beyond that it's full of overgrown bushes. It's a bit of a jungle, and Gran says we should try harder to keep it tidy, but mostly we like it that way. Especially Wild Thing. (I suppose a jungle is the right place for a Wild Thing, come to think of it.)

There was no sign of Wild Thing, and I reckoned she was hiding.

"Josephine, come here this moment!" said Dad crossly, striding across the grass. Then he stopped short. "What's this sheet doing in my vegetable patch?"

The sheet was spread out across the bare earth in front of us, a bit like a picnic blanket.

"Has it blown off the washing line?" Gran wondered aloud.

I thought they were both being silly.

"Wild Thing took it, just now! And I tried to stop her!"

"The naughty child!" said Gran. "I assumed she was hanging it out to dry."

I shook my head. Honestly. You'd think Gran would know by now that "helpful" is not my sister's middle name.

Dad put his hands round his mouth like a loudspeaker. "WILD THING, COME HERE THIS MINUTE!"

There was a tiny pause. Then Wild Thing's head suddenly popped out of the ground at our feet. "No need to shout," she said.

It was a bit of a shock seeing my sister come out of nowhere like that. "What are you doing down there?" I demanded. "And . . . where is the rest of you?"

"In my new den, of course," said Wild Thing. And she disappeared again, under the sheet.

Dad gave a roar of annoyance. Then he knelt down and grabbed a corner of the sheet – and pulled.

Wild Thing gave a howl. "Stop!" she bellowed. "That's my roof!"

As the sheet came away, we could see my sister crouched in a big hole in the ground. Next to her was Hound Dog. He obviously thought Dad grabbing the sheet was a game, because he immediately grabbed the other end with his teeth. The more my dad pulled *one* end of the sheet, the more Hound Dog tugged on the other. After a few seconds there was a RIPPING noise, and Dad was left holding one corner, while Hound Dog went dancing off round the garden with the rest.

"This sheet is ruined!" yelled Dad.

"My *roof* is ruined!" wailed Wild Thing. "What will keep out the rain now?"

She glowered at Dad like it was his fault. Then she began clambering out of the hole.

"Honestly, Josephine!" said Gran. "You're filthy!"

She was, too. She looked like a Swamp Monster emerging from the mud.

"It's a really big hole," I said, peering into it. I was quite impressed. "Did you dig it yourself?"

"Hound Dog helped," said my sister. "He likes to dig."

"Actually, *I* dug most of it," said Dad. "And back-breaking work it was, too."

"Really," said Gran disapprovingly. "I'd have thought you'd have better things to do, Tom, than waste your time digging holes for Josephine to hide in."

Dad went red with annoyance. "I didn't dig it for *her*. I dug it as a trench to plant potatoes. I didn't know I was going to get a – a – a squatter!"

I giggled. I wasn't sure exactly what a squatter was, but I reckoned the word summed up Wild Thing pretty well, as she sat squatting in the mud.

"Anyway," Gran pressed on, "obviously Josephine's going to need a bath, and I'm afraid that sheet is probably past repair. But first – and most important – *what has happened to my handbag?*"

Dad and I had forgotten about Gran's handbag. Wild Thing didn't say anything, so I said, "Wild Thing – have *you* seen it?"

"No," said my sister. She had a stubborn look on her face. "Not seen bag."

I was suspicious. I went and peered into her muddy hole.

"What's that?" I asked, pointing at a rather grubby – yet familiar – object, half hidden by a pile of Wild Thing's toys.

Wild Thing howled and dived for it. "That's mine!" she shrieked. Then she bounded out of her pit again, clutching Gran's once smart and shiny, now *very* muddy, handbag.

"No, it's not, it's my new handbag! Give it here!" Gran made a grab for Wild Thing, who dodged.

"It's not a *bag*!"

"What is it, then?" asked Dad.

"It's my worm house!"

"Your *what*?" Gran went all mean and frozen-looking. Like a granny version of Narnia's White Witch.

"My worm house! My worms need somewhere to live. It's their own little home."

Gran gave a sort of wordless gasp. Then she grabbed the handbag.

"Ugh! It's full of soil!"

She turned it upside down and a shower of earth and twigs fell to the ground. So did at least ten wriggling, squirming worms.

"Poor little things!" shrieked Wild Thing, and she tried to grab the bag, but Dad grabbed her first and that was the end of that.

"It was very wrong of you to take Gran's handbag," he told my sister. "I know you wanted to make a home for your worms, but that doesn't excuse it."

"And where are all my things?" demanded Gran. "My purse, my keys, my phone, my glasses. . ."

We soon found out where they were. Wild Thing had emptied them into the compost bin. Gran was furious, and after she had picked them out from among the eggshells and bits of old grass clippings, she gave Wild Thing a piece of her mind. Dad said she had every right to be angry. He sent Wild Thing to her room in disgrace.

I couldn't help finding it funny though. Only Wild Thing would try and turn a handbag into a worm house!

3

Wild Thing was allowed down again for tea. Gran had gone home by then, but Wild Thing was in a terrible sulk about the collapse of her "lovely den", as she called it. She kept going on about it, in between slipping Hound Dog bits of bacon under the table.

"My poor worms. They're going to be all cold!"

"Nonsense," said Dad. "They're earthworms. And what earthworms like best is being in the *earth*. Not in handbags. Not in your jeans pockets. Earth."

Wild Thing wouldn't agree though.

"Going to make a new den," she announced, through a mouthful of tomato.

"Not in my potato trench, you're not," said

Dad sternly. "The only thing that's going to live there is potatoes!"

But when Wild Thing gets an idea into her head, she doesn't let go of it easily.

Dad usually describes this as "a phase she's going through". She's had a lot of "phases" in her time, and they've all been awful.

There was the phase when she kept sticking things down her ear.

The phase when she kept sticking things down *other people's* ears.

The phase when she started writing on walls. JOSEPHINE IS BESTEST BEETS THE RESTEST is *not* what you want to find on your bedroom wall, in luminous, glow-in-the-dark pen. Until Dad got round to painting it out, I used to have to look at it *every single night*.

Wild Thing's new phase was all about dens and camping out. I reckoned Wild Thing had got the idea after seeing some photos of her best friend Max's last camping trip. The fact that her class were doing *The Jungle Book* as a play at school didn't help either. It had given Wild Thing the idea that it would be really great to live in a den in the woods.

"She'll soon get over it," Dad told me, after he had sent Wild Thing off to get ready for her much-needed bath.

I wasn't so sure.

I went to watch TV in the front room, and forgot about my sister. Hound Dog came with me. He likes watching TV. Actually, I'm not sure he's bothered about what's on the screen (unless it's a dog food advert) but he loves curling up on the sofa with whoever is watching television and having his tummy tickled.

Eventually Dad put his head round the door and said, "Have you done your homework?" and of course I hadn't, and I hadn't done my guitar practice either. So I got up and went upstairs, with Hound Dog lolloping beside me.

I tiptoed past Wild Thing's door (I'd had about enough of my sister for one day). It was covered in glitter, chewing gum, splodges of paint, Hound Dog's paw prints, and five socks that Wild Thing superglued there one Saturday afternoon when she was feeling bored.(The socks were "in case Santa came early" she explained to Dad afterwards.)

I reached my own bedroom door. The only thing it has on it is a sign saying KEEP OUT! (WILD THING, THAT MEANS YOU!)

I opened my door. Then I just stood there on the threshold, gasping with shock.

I hardly recognized my room.

My stripy duvet had been chucked in a corner. So had my stuffed toys.

My bed had completely vanished, under a lopsided pole (the mop, I suspected) with my stripy sheet draped all over it. It looked like a ship in full sail. Or a circus tent gone wonky.

My fluffy rug had been pushed aside. Instead, there was a pile of old wood in the middle of the floor. I recognized it as the driftwood that Wild Thing and I had gathered on the beach last summer, plus some sticks that Wild Thing collected last time we went to the park. As I stared, an earwig came crawling out from under one of them!

Most mysterious of all was the packet of sausages poking out from inside my bedroom slipper.

Only one person could be responsible for this.

"Wild Thing!" I snarled.

My sister stuck her head out from under the sheet.

"Hello, Kate."

"What do you think you're doing?"

"I'm camping," Wild Thing said, as if it were the most obvious thing in the world. "This is my tent."

"But – you know you're not allowed in my bedroom!"

"There isn't anywhere else."

"Yes, there is. *Your* room!"

Wild Thing looked at me as if I was stupid. "I can't camp out in *my own bedroom*. Where's the point in that?"

"Well, you're not to camp out in my bedroom either. It's not a campsite."

Wild Thing heaved a sigh. "I guess I'll move everything to Dad's bedroom then."

"You'd better not," I warned her. I stepped forward and almost tripped over the pile of wood. "What's this for?"

"That's my campfire," Wild Thing said. "I'm going to roast sausages."

"You are *not* roasting sausages in *my* bedroom!"

"Yes, I am. Hey, you – give those back. Bad dog!"

This last bit wasn't to me. She was talking to Hound Dog, who was standing wagging his tail with the packet of sausages in his mouth. He quickly dived behind the wardrobe where she couldn't get at him!

"And you know you are NEVER, EVER allowed to play with matches!"

"I'm not going to use matches," said Wild Thing. "Look."

She knelt down by the "campfire". (Hound

Dog kept a wary eye on her from behind the wardrobe.) Then she picked up two sticks and started rubbing them together. "See?" she said. "Like this."

I was relieved. I reckoned Wild Thing wasn't going to start a fire by rubbing sticks together, even if she kept it up for the next year. On the other hand, she was making a right mess of my floor. There was bark and moss everywhere.

"Stop that now!"

Wild Thing ignored me.

I reached a decision. "Dad!" I bellowed at the top of my voice.

When Dad arrived, we managed to catch Hound Dog and wrestle the sausages away from him. Then we dismantled Wild Thing's "tent" (ignoring Wild Thing's protests) and got my room back to its usual state. Dad also had a very serious talk with Wild Thing about fire safety, and respecting other people's space (the other people being me!).He also forbade her from making any more dens – or campsites – inside the house.

"Can we go camping *outdoors* then?" asked Wild Thing. "In a real tent?"

"Weeeell lll. . ." said Dad. He didn't sound keen.

"Want to meet bears," Wild Thing explained.

"Like *The Jungle Book*."

"But there aren't any bears near us," Dad said.

"Wolves, then."

"There aren't any wolves either."

"What about panthers?"

"There's certainly no panthers."

Wild Thing made a face. You could tell she didn't believe Dad. Then she turned to me. "You'd like to go camping, wouldn't you, Kate?"

Actually, she was right. Much as I hated to admit it, for once my sister had made a good suggestion. "Go on, Dad," I coaxed. "I'd *love* to go camping. And you've never taken us. Besides, just think, if there *are* any wolves or panthers, they might eat Wild Thing!"

"Tempting though that is," said Dad, "we haven't got a tent." I think he was making excuses.

"We could borrow Bonnie's. Her family have got a great tent."

Dad made a face. "I'll think about it," he said. Which is what he always says when actually he's planning to forget about whatever it is as soon as possible.

"Don't *think* about it," said Wild Thing. "Do it!"

"Yes," I agreed. "We could take Hound Dog – he'd love it. We could go hiking and exploring, and at night we could have a real campfire, and cook things."

"Sausages," said Wild Thing at once. Hound Dog wagged his tail and whined.

"It sounds lovely," said Dad, "but let me tell you, camping isn't like that. It's all wet socks and soggy sleeping bags and hard rocks sticking into your back at night, and having to wade miles through a muddy field to take a shower."

"Wonderful," said Wild Thing enthusiastically. "When can we go?"

Dad groaned. "I do a lot of things for you girls. But I'm not leaving my comfortable, warm bed to sleep in a muddy field in a leaky old tent. And that's final!"

And however much we begged and argued, he wouldn't change his mind.

The next morning, on the way to school, I told my friend Bonnie all about Wild Thing and her "camping out".

"I'd love to go on a real camping trip," I said wistfully.

"Maybe Mum will let you come with us some time," said Bonnie. "Although it is a bit of a squeeze already, to be honest." Bonnie has two older brothers, Zach and Harris, *and* two enormous dogs, Sugar and Sweet, so I could imagine there wouldn't be much room.

I forgot all about camping when we reached our classroom. For there, sitting on a desk, was a new girl. I immediately felt sure it was Fiona.

She was very pretty. She had honey-blonde hair, and it fell just so – I've never understood how people get their hair to do that. And although she was only wearing ordinary school clothes, somehow her socks looked whiter and her shirt crisper than everyone else's. She seemed just the sort of girl that Gran would think was marvellous.

She was chatting with Helena and Carina, who are probably the two girls in our class that I like least. She kept nodding and giggling, and every now and then she would flick back her hair.

"Who's that?" asked Bonnie, nudging me.

I explained. "Come on," I added, remembering my promise to Gran. "We'd better say hello."

Somehow, I really didn't feel like it. But a promise is a promise. So we went over. They were chatting hard and didn't notice me. I had to cough several times. Loudly.

"Umm, hello," I said, when they finally turned round to look at me. "Are you Fiona? I'm Kate."

"Oh. Hello, Kate." She didn't sound warm, though. And her eyes were going up and down me instead of staying on my face, as if she were checking out the fact that my shoes were a bit scuffed and my cardigan had ink on it.

"Our grans are good friends," I went on. "So I just wanted to say – umm – welcome to the school."

They all just stared at me. I began to feel really awkward. Like I had said something really stupid. Then they began to giggle.

"That's nice that your grans are friends," sniggered Carina. "Maybe you'll all hang out together. And do some knitting!"

They screeched with laughter, like this was the best joke ever. I went red. Actually, Gran *does* like to knit. She's taught me how, and I'm making Dad a scarf for his birthday. What's wrong with that?

I took a deep breath and lifted my chin. "Well, if there's anything you need – like someone to show you round – just let me know," I said, with dignity. Then I turned round to leave, only unfortunately I tripped over my shoelace. Which wasn't very dignified at all. Carina, Fiona and Helena thought it was hilarious, of course.

"Meanies," muttered Bonnie, as we moved away. "Don't you worry about them, Kate."

I was pleased to find that our teacher, Miss Deng, wasn't impressed with Fiona either. She's usually extra-nice to new kids, but after Fiona had yawned loudly and flicked her hair back for about the one hundred and ninety-ninth time in the middle of maths, Miss Deng snapped, "Fiona, stop playing with your hair! I don't want to tell you again!"

I didn't expect to have much more to do with Fiona. But at the very end of the afternoon, during library time, Fiona came up to the table where I was reading. To my surprise, she gave me a friendly smile. Then she said, "I remember now, Grandma *has* mentioned your family, Kate. Your dad is some kind of musician, isn't he?"

"He's a guitarist." I gave her a little smile. She was looking so friendly I reckoned maybe she wasn't as bad as I'd thought.

"I heard your dad was in a band once," Fiona continued. "What's it called?"

"Monkey Magic, and—"

"What a funny name."

I was going to say I didn't see anything funny about it, but before I could, Fiona said, "It's such a shame he never made the big time."

"How do you mean?" I asked.

"Well, you know. *I've* never even *heard* of Monkey Magic. It's a shame he's all washed up."

I gasped. There were quite a lot of things I could have said in response. Like, for example:

1) Monkey Magic *are* big. *Lots* of people have heard of them! (Even if Fiona hasn't!)

2) It's true Dad's not really in Monkey Magic any more. But that's not because he's "washed up". It's because he's busy bringing up Wild Thing and me. He says being a dad and playing in a rock band don't mix.

3) Even though he's not a full-time member of the band, he still writes most of their songs. Wes and the other guys are always begging him to perform with them. He's been on TV loads of times, and to America, and if he wanted, he could play all over the world!

But as you've probably found, it's lots easier to think what you should have said *afterwards*. At that moment, all these thoughts were jumbled up in my head, so that all I could actually say, in a sort of high-pitched squeak, was, "He's not washed up!"

"Oh, sorry, I shouldn't have said *washed up*," said Fiona at once. She gave me a sugary smile. I think she really was *meaning* to be nice. "I just meant it's a shame he never became a success. And if I ever do decide to take up the guitar, I'll definitely come to him for my lessons."

"I'm sure he'd *love* that," I said. I was meaning to be sarcastic. But I don't think Fiona got it, because she went right on smiling. You'd think her jaw would have been getting tired by now.

"And it must be so hard for both of you," she went on, "looking after your sister. I've heard she's a real handful."

"What do you mean?" I said, bristling.

"Well . . . the things people say about her. She sounds out of control."

"That's ridiculous," I snapped. "Wild Thing – I mean, Josephine – isn't out of control. She's just *little*, that's all. Really, she's just like any other five-year-old."

"Well—" began Fiona, obviously about to argue. But then she broke off and said, "What's that noise?"

For the last few minutes, there'd been the sound of voices from outside. I'd thought at first it was just the younger children in the playground – they always get out of school a few minutes before us. But they didn't usually make that much noise.

A horrible suspicion crept into my mind. *Please* don't let it be her, I thought. . .

Because whenever there's trouble, Wild Thing is sure to be involved!

5

As I went out into the playground, I saw a big crowd of people gathered near the doors where the Little Ones come out. All the noise seemed to be coming from that direction. I ran to see what was going on.

"Please let me through," I begged, wriggling my way around prams, parents and lots of little kids who were pushing and shoving at one another to try and get the best view. At last I reached the front of the crowd.

Oh no! My heart dropped like a stone. *There* was Wild Thing, just as I'd feared – right in the middle of things, as usual! And she wasn't alone. While everybody watched, she and another little girl were circling around each other and jabbing the air with their clenched fists, like a pair of boxers about to attack. At the same time they were bawling at the tops of their voices.

"I'm going to be Baloo!"

"No, I'm going to be Baloo!"

"No, I'm going to be Baloo, so there!"

The other girl had honey-blonde hair tied back into bunches with big white bows. Her shoes were ultra shiny. Her clothes were spotless. All in all, it didn't take much to work out that this was Fiona's little sister, Nerisa.

"Now calm down," I began.

They ignored me.

"*Of course* I'm going to be Baloo," said Wild Thing in a loud voice. "I'm a great bear!" And she got down on all fours and began snuffling around the way a bear would snuffle. Then she bared her teeth and gave a big, deep, chesty bear *growwwwlll*.

Everyone looked astonished, even frightened, except for Nerisa, who just stood there with her mouth pursed. I thought this might be a good

moment to get hold of Wild Thing. So I edged
towards her, but she saw me coming and crawled
away round the other side of Nerisa.

"Kate? Whatever is going on?" It was Fiona. I
tried not to meet her eyes. I knew exactly what
she was thinking: *Just like any other five-year-old,
eh?* And she was right!

"Wild Thing, get up!" I tried to grab my sister again but she snarled at me and began to shamble around the playground. She did look quite like a bear, I have to admit.

Nerisa raised her voice. "Of course *I'm* being Baloo," she said. "Mummy says I'm a wonderful actress!"

Gran came hurrying up. "I'm so sorry I'm late," she puffed. She looked around, saw Wild Thing on the ground, and said in a sharp voice, "Josephine, get up at once!"

"Hello, Mrs Brent," said Fiona. As soon as Gran saw her a big smile appeared on her face, like a light bulb flashing on.

"*Hello*, dear," she said in a completely different tone of voice. "And little Nerisa too. How lovely to see you both. I do hope you're settling in?"

Fiona smiled prettily and said yes, Mrs Brent, they were, thank you very much. (Nerisa was still glowering at Wild Thing.)

"And you've met Kate, of course," Gran gushed. "I hope she's been looking after you."

"Oh, yes, Mrs Brent," cooed Fiona, smiling and nodding like a little doll.

I thought this yucky conversation might go on for ever. But at that moment there was an interruption, when Nerisa squealed loudly.

"What's the matter?" asked Fiona.

"She bit me! She bit me on the ankle!"

"Did not!" Wild Thing shouted.

"Then what *were* you doing, crawling around Nerisa's feet?" demanded Gran crossly.

"Being a bear," said Wild Thing.

"Are you *sure* you didn't bite her?"

"NO! DIDN'T!" There was a long pause. "Maybe just a nibble."

Gran looked ready to explode. She snatched hold of Wild Thing's hand and pulled her to her feet.

"Get up this minute! Why can't you behave?" She stared after Fiona and Nerisa, who were now heading off towards the school gates. "What lovely manners they have. What a very nice pair of girls!"

I don't think either Wild Thing or I agreed with that!

On the way home, I finally worked out what the "bear" thing was all about. Miss Randolph, who teaches the Little Ones, was going to choose who would have which part in their play of *The Jungle Book*. Wild Thing was desperate to be Baloo the Bear. The trouble was, so was Nerisa.

"You'll just have to see what your teacher decides," said Gran.

"But I *am* a bear!" said Wild Thing. "And Nissa's just a rotten old snake!"

Now, Wild Thing is a terrible show-off in my opinion, and I don't like to encourage her. Furthermore, I'm not the biggest fan of my sister's performances. (That time she watched *Mamma Mia* on the telly and then burst into my bedroom and started singing Abba songs to all my friends, wearing her pink wig and wedgy boots and *nothing else*, was still fresh in my mind.) *But* I have to admit I thought she'd make a better bear than Nerisa.

"That Nerisa's too clean and tidy to be a bear," I said.

"Oh, I don't know," said Gran. "There's nothing wrong with being clean and tidy. I just wish Josephine would follow her example." And she looked at Wild Thing – who had mud all over her hands and knees from crawling around the playground, and a crisp packet stuck behind one ear – and sighed.

On Friday evening, while I was doing my maths homework, Dad had a call from Wes, the lead singer of Monkey Magic. Dad was loading up the dishwasher at the time, so he put the call on the speakerphone. This meant I heard everything.

"We've got a few gigs coming up," Wes said, after they had chatted for a bit. "And we've just said yes to being lead act at Brammingham Rock Festival. Do you remember Brammingham?"

"Cool place," Dad said. "I always enjoyed playing there."

"Yeah . . . so, anyhow, we've a lot to sort out. I want to work on that new song you wrote – do you think you could make it to rehearsal tomorrow?"

Dad ummed and ahhed for a bit, but eventually he said he would try to come. When he'd put down the phone, he finished clearing the kitchen. Then he called Gran.

This time he didn't put the call on speakerphone, so I could only hear Dad's side of things, as he asked if she could look after Wild Thing and me the next day.

"Thanks, Mum," I heard him say at last, "you're a lifesaver. If you could be here at ten, I can make the start of the rehearsal. Of course, there is just one thing you might have forgotten . . . tomorrow is Clementine's party."

There was a long pause. Then even I could hear the squawking from the other end of the phone!

Dad hung up at last and turned to me. "She's agreed!" he said cheerfully. "Not that she's happy about it. Let's just hope Wild Thing behaves herself."

What I hadn't reckoned on was that *I* would have to go to Clementine's party as well. I'd been planning to go round to Bonnie's. But at the last moment, Bonnie's mum had decided they'd visit relatives that weekend. All my other friends were busy too.

"But I don't want to go to a party full of five-year-olds," I complained. "It'll be awful!"

"You'll be good company for me, Kate," said Gran, giving my arm a squeeze, as we waited in the hall for Wild Thing. "Now, where's your sister? We don't want to be late."

At that moment, Wild Thing came bounding down the stairs. She was holding Clementine's present. But it wasn't looking the way it had ten minutes ago, when *I* had finished wrapping it for her. Now the wrapping paper was wrinkly and the big bow had collapsed.

"What have you done to it?" I demanded.

"Nothing."

"Nothing?"

"Well . . . it fell in the bath."

"In the *bath*? Why were you taking a bath?"

"I wasn't taking a bath."

"So how did it fall in?" (I was beginning to think that either me or Wild Thing was going crazy.)

"*Peter Rabbit* was having a bath," Wild Thing explained, waving her cuddly toy. (At least, he *had* been cuddly. Now he was dripping wet.) "It's his fault, really."

"Never mind that," Gran interrupted. "What *I* want to know is why you're dressed as a dog."

"Not a *dog*," said Wild Thing indignantly. "I'm a bear! Can't you tell?" She gave a deep growl.

Gran said she didn't care what kind of animal Wild Thing was meant to be, she wasn't going like that to the party. Then she marched her upstairs. I could hear a lot of arguing, but I guess Gran won, because when they came back Wild Thing was dressed as I'd never seen her before. She had on a pink dress with ruffles that Gran once gave her, and a little pink cardigan with ribbon bows, and dainty princess sandals from the dressing-up box. To top it all off, she was carrying a shiny plastic handbag.

47

She was also scowling like she wanted to bite somebody!

"Is that what you're wearing?" I asked doubtfully.

"Yes!" Wild Thing shouted. She pointed at Gran. "*She* made me!"

"I think she looks *lovely*," said Gran approvingly.

"Just like a little girl *should* look, going to a party. Such a nice change from jeans."

I shrugged, and we all set off for the party. When we got to Clementine's house, though, we had a bit of a surprise. Nobody was there. Gran said crossly, "I do hope we haven't got the wrong day!" But when I looked at the invitation, I realized that it wasn't the wrong *day*, but the wrong *place*.

"The party's not here."

"Oh really," said Gran crossly. "I'm sure I checked the address on the invitation."

"It did say we could *meet* here," I said, "but the party's actually at the park. I think they've already left."

"That's right," said Wild Thing cheerfully. "In the park. Near the woods."

So we drove to the park. When we got there, we soon found the other children running around under the trees, playing hide-and-seek. Of course, they were all wearing jeans and hoodies and trainers. Unlike Wild Thing, who was wearing *exactly* the wrong clothes for a trip to the park.

"Well, it's too late now," said Gran when I pointed this out.

Wild Thing wasn't worried. She dumped her soggy present with Clementine's other gifts and ran off to join her friends under the trees. Gran sat down with some of the other children's parents at a picnic table and started chatting. I drifted away as far as I could from the party. I was wishing I'd brought Hound Dog. He always loves going to the park.

Soon Clementine's mother was calling the children for the party games. They didn't seem very interested until she brought out a piñata – a big, colourful paper donkey stuffed full of sweets that she hung from the branch of a tree. All the children took turns clumping it with an enormous plastic mallet.

Of course, it had to be Wild Thing who ended up clumping Clementine (the Birthday Girl) on the head.

I was watching the whole thing and I reckon it wasn't entirely Wild Thing's fault. For one thing, I think *really* she was aiming for Nerisa, and only clumped Clementine by mistake when Nerisa ducked. And I reckon Nerisa asked for it, because she kept trying to grab an extra turn hitting the donkey. And anyway, the mallet was only made of plastic, and I don't think it could have hurt *that* much.

On the other hand, it *was* Wild Thing's fault that when Clementine's mother tried to take the mallet off her, she howled and stamped and wouldn't give it back. And then, when Clementine's mother *did* grab hold of the mallet and pull, Wild Thing let go very suddenly, so that Clementine's mother fell backwards and sat down with a thud in the dirt. And when Gran clocked what was going on and came striding over roaring, "Josephine, you come here this minute!" Wild Thing *didn't* come here. Instead she ran off into the woods yelling, "Not coming! Not playing any more with stupid donkey!" And as she couldn't run very well in the dainty sandals, she just took them off and threw them away and went barefoot, yelling, "Can't catch me!"

So there you go. A typical birthday party with Wild Thing. Instead of a sweet little gathering of five-year-olds, she'd turned it into a full-blown riot!

Gran was standing at the edge of the woods with her hands on her hips, shouting, "Josephine! Don't you dare ignore me!" Meanwhile I was trying to pretend I wasn't there.

It didn't work.

"Your sister is awful, isn't she?" said an amused voice.

I turned around. *Fiona.* Just about the last person that I wanted to see!

"Oh, hello," I said.

Fiona sat down next to me – after taking a very long time checking the fallen tree I was sitting on to make sure there were no bits of dirt or creepy crawlies to spoil her immaculate leggings.

"Wherever there's trouble, you're sure to find her!" said Fiona, turning to me with a smile. "Josephine Brent!"

She was right. I often think the same thing myself. But that doesn't mean I liked Fiona saying it!

"*Your* sister gets involved too," I pointed out. "She was screaming at the top of her voice just now. I think some of it was actually her fault."

"Oh, no," said Fiona. "Nerisa's never to blame." She wasn't annoyed or upset by what I'd said – just convinced that she knew best. It made me grate my teeth.

"Grandma says she feels really sorry for your grandmother sometimes, having to deal with your sister," Fiona went on.

"Oh, does she," I muttered, but I guess Fiona didn't hear me.

"And now that Nerisa is going to play Baloo the bear . . . that's going to annoy your sister. But it's silly of her to think she owns the part. After all, Nerisa is a wonderful actress."

I looked at her in surprise. "What do you mean? How come you think Nerisa's got the part?"

"Because her teacher mentioned it confidentially to my mum. She wanted to make sure Nerisa could cope with it, being so new."

I sighed. Wild Thing was going to be mad as a wasp about that.

"You know, Kate. . ." Fiona flicked back her hair and looked at me sideways.

"What?"

"Well, don't take this the wrong way, but . . . don't you think you should make some friends your own age? Instead of tagging along with your little sister?"

I couldn't believe her nerve. "I've got *plenty* of friends my own age! Anyway, you're here too!"

"Not really." Fiona flicked her hair again. "I'm on the way to my piano lesson. Have *you* ever thought of learning to play an instrument?"

"Well – you see—" I was going to say that I've

been playing guitar and saxophone for ages, and actually, for my age, I'm pretty good. But Fiona didn't wait for me to finish.

"If you do, you'll have to practise *really* hard and not get discouraged," she told me. (Like she was a grown-up talking to a little kid!) "It's easy to start but the thing is to keep going. Little and often! That's what my piano teacher says."

She was leaning back a bit, and I was really tempted to give her a good shove, so that she fell right into the dirt. But at that moment I heard Gran calling me.

"I'm sorry to call you away when you and Fiona are having such a nice chat," Gran said. (*A nice chat?* Did she have eyes?) "But I need you to help me find Josephine. It's time for the party tea and I'm beginning to get worried."

I grumbled a bit, but I reckoned it was better than hanging out with Fiona, so I went into the trees to look for my missing sister.

"Wild Thing!" I yelled at the top of my voice. "Where are you?"

No answer.

"Wild Thing, it's teatime!"

Silence.

"There's lemonade! And marshmallows!"

I was sure that would bring my greedy sister running. But there was still no answer.

I wondered if she had decided to make a den, as she loves dens so much, and had forgotten about the party. So I got down and started peering behind trees and boulders. I got very scratched, and my knees were covered in mud. But there was no sign of Wild Thing.

Maybe she had found a cave deep in the woods, I thought, and we would *never* find her. She would live among the trees, eating berries and nuts like a wild bear. The police would go looking for her . . . *everyone* would be looking for her . . . but she'd be lost for ever.

Good.

I crawled out from under the trees. The other children were all sitting at a picnic table, eating the birthday tea. One of them got up and came towards me. It was Wild Thing's best friend, Max.

"Oh, Kate," he moaned (Max is a real moaner), "where's Josephine? Have the bears got her?"

"Of course they haven't. There aren't any bears."

"Josephine says there are."

"Then Josephine is wrong."

"Josephine's never wrong," said Max solemnly.

I giggled. Max was going to get a lot of shocks in his life if he thought that!

"Would you like *me* to help look for Josephine?" It was Nerisa, who had suddenly appeared at my elbow.

"Err . . . well. . ." I said doubtfully.

"I think we should tell her she's going to be Bagheera the Panther in our class play," said Nerisa. "She wanted to be Baloo, but *I'm* doing that, because I'm such a good actress. But I'm sure she'll love being a panther."

I was fairly sure she wouldn't!

"What's that noise?" asked Max.

I stopped and listened. "I don't hear any—"
But then I did hear it. A rustling from somewhere amongst the trees.

"It's probably just a squirrel," I said. But I moved towards the noise, and Max and Nerisa followed me. We stopped under a large beech tree.

"I can't hear anything," said Nerisa, after a pause.

"I can!" Max looked round nervously.

I put my finger to my lips. "Shhh . . . be as quiet as you can and *listen*!"

There was another rustling and this time something else – a sort of low snarling.

Now, squirrels don't snarl.

"Wild Thing, come out this minute!" I kicked at the nearest pile of leaves, but there was no sign of a squirrel or my sister. Then I heard the snarling again. It sounded very close.

"M-m-maybe there's a big dog," said Nerisa.

She actually sounded anxious. "Maybe it's going to jump out at us."

"Maybe it's a bear!" Max said.

"There are no bears!" I was sure it must be Wild Thing. But I looked all around the tree trunk and I couldn't see any sign of her.

Then I heard it again. And I realized something. The snarling was coming from *above* us.

I looked up, just in time to make out a dark shape through the leaves – and then, with a yowl, it leapt from its branch and dropped like a stone right on top of Nerisa.

"Well, she did say I was a panther," said Wild Thing. "And that's what panthers do. They hide in trees, and then *jump* on you!"

We were back home, telling the story to Dad. Gran had dumped us on the doorstep and driven off, having told Dad first that she would NEVER, EVER, in any circumstances, take Wild Thing to a birthday party again. "I feel I've aged ten years!" she'd declared as she slammed the car door.

Wild Thing stood in the middle of the kitchen floor, dripping moss, leaves and twigs in equal amounts. Her once pretty dress was ripped and stained, there was a big scratch on her cheek and her bare feet were coated in mud.

She refused to admit she had done anything wrong. And much to my annoyance, Dad didn't even tell her off much. In fact, he was quite cheerful. I reckoned he was just pleased he had missed the party!

"Nerisa could have been seriously hurt," I scolded.

"She's horrible," said Wild Thing. "If I was really a panther, I'd eat her for dinner."

"Now, now," said Dad.

"'Now, now'?" I echoed. "Is that *all* you've got to say? How about straight to bed with no supper? How about no TV for a week? How about. . ."

But Dad reckoned it wasn't that serious. He said that climbing trees, and jumping out of them, was just the sort of thing that kids *should* get up to. He certainly had when he was a boy. "Good, healthy, outdoor play. So much better than being hunched over a screen!"

That was easy for *him* to say. *He* hadn't been there. He hadn't had to listen to all the parents complaining. And he wouldn't have to go to school on Monday either, where everybody would be talking about it (Fiona would make sure of that!).

"Oh, nobody will blame you, Kate," he said. "They know you're the sensible one."

"That's what you think!"

I was getting a bit fed up with being the sensible one, if you want to know the truth.

"Just chill out a bit," Dad told me.

"Yes, well, just wait until you have to take her to a party. Come to think of it, I'm sure there was an envelope in her bag yesterday. Maybe it's another invitation!"

That rattled Dad all right. He rushed off to find Wild Thing's school bag and came back holding an envelope.

"Doesn't look like an invitation," said Dad, ripping it open.

"Maybe it's one of those letters to say she's got nits," I said. "In fact, I'm sure I can see something crawling in her hair now. Oh, no, wait . . . it's a caterpillar."

Wild Thing was really pleased about the caterpillar. She went off to look for a jam jar for it to live in. Meanwhile, Dad glanced at the letter, laughed, and tossed it aside.

I picked it up.

Dear Parent,

We would like to inform you that your daughter has been selected to have violin lessons. If you would like to take up this opportunity . . . and it went on to explain about prices, and how to hire a violin.

I frowned. "So will she have lessons?" I asked Dad, who was now shaking out Wild Thing's bag into the bin. (Honestly, it gets horrible in there. Bits of old Play-Doh, crisps, pebbles, snail shells and leaves and twigs from the playground. Once Dad claimed he'd found *a mouse.*)

"No way is Wild Thing learning the violin," Dad said. "I mean, just think about it."

I thought about it. I could imagine Wild Thing *sitting* on a violin and breaking it, or bashing somebody over the head with it, or enjoying a game of tug-the-violin with Hound Dog. I couldn't imagine her actually playing one.

And suddenly I felt relieved. I realized I didn't want Wild Thing to play the violin. I suppose it's because music has always been *my* thing, not Wild Thing's – well, mine and Dad's. Even if it was selfish of me, I just didn't want Wild Thing muscling in.

But I didn't feel relieved for long, because when Wild Thing came back in a few minutes later and heard about the letter, she said, "I *want* to play the violin. And I'm going to play the violin. So there!"

"*Bears* don't play the violin," I said, very cunningly I thought.

"They do if they're joining a circus!" replied Wild Thing.

I thought it might actually be worth Wild Thing playing a violin if she went off to join a circus. But Dad said, "You are not taking up the violin, and that's that."

Wild Thing glowered. "Am so!"

"Are not!"

"Kate plays things," said Wild Thing. "She plays saxophone and guitar. So why can't I play the violin?"

"That's different," I said.

Wild Thing lost her temper then, and started

shouting and stamping, and Dad sent her to her room. However, once she had gone, he said to me, "I suppose we'll have to let her learn the violin if she really wants to."

"Why?" (I *definitely* didn't agree!)

"Well, if she's that keen . . . I just wish she'd chosen a different instrument. Violin sounds dreadful when a beginner plays it – like a cat being strangled. Maybe I should offer to teach her the guitar instead."

"No!" I jumped up from the floor, where I'd been stroking Hound Dog. "The guitar is *my* thing. Not hers!"

"All right, Kate," said Dad, rather surprised. "Violin it is, then. But there's no need to get upset. I thought you'd be more sensible than—"

I didn't let him finish. "I've had about enough of being sensible," I told him. "Wild Thing is never sensible – and she always gets her own way!" I lifted my chin and swept out of the room with as much dignity as I could. Or that's what I meant to do. Unfortunately, my grand exit was ruined when I tripped over Hound Dog. He leapt up with a volley of barks, and I went staggering across the rug and almost fell over.

I'd hoped to show Dad how offended I was, but I think I heard him laughing as I marched into the hall.

On Sunday night we went out for a pizza with Wes and Luke, who are both members of Monkey Magic. Wes is a good friend of Dad's, and Hound Dog used to be his dog before he came to live with us. I love going for pizza, but I was still feeling a bit moody. I felt even worse when Wes and Luke made a big fuss of Wild Thing and her new violin. "Maybe you should get an *electric* violin!" Wes told her.

Oh, great. Then she'd sound like a strangled cat, only ten times as loud.

I tried telling them about the latest piece I was learning on my saxophone, but they were too busy chuckling away at Wild Thing's choice of pizza toppings: banana, tuna and honey. ("Because those are all things bears like," Wild Thing explained.)

"What a kid!" Wes kept saying as Wild Thing gobbled it down.

I cut up my cheese and tomato pizza and said nothing.

For dessert, Wild Thing chose vanilla ice cream topped with chocolate sauce, marshmallows . . . and olives. Yes, *olives*. Everyone thought that was even more hilarious.

Nobody seemed interested in the chocolate fudge cake *I* was eating.

Then Wes started talking about the rock festival that he and the rest of Monkey Magic were going to be performing at in a few weeks' time. "It's going to be great!" he said.

"What's a rock fessell?" asked Wild Thing through a mouthful of ice cream.

"It's where a lot of music fans go and camp out for a weekend and listen to bands," Dad explained. "Usually it's somewhere like a stately home, or a farm, where there's lots of space. There's a campsite and also lots of big marquees and stages where the bands play."

It turned out Dad knew all about rock festivals because when he was younger he and the rest of Monkey Magic had often gone off together in a rickety old van, to play at them. They had performed, and listened to other bands, and camped out in a muddy field with lots of other festival-goers.

"Camping," said Wild Thing. Her eyes lit up.

"Yes, those were the days," said Wes nostalgically. "And Brammingham was always one of the best. In fact –" he turned to Dad "– why don't you all come along?"

"Yeah," agreed Luke, "And then you can play with the band – just like old times."

I looked at Dad pleadingly. Music *and* camping – it sounded wonderful to me. Wild Thing was so excited she was dribbling her ice cream.

"The answer's no," said Dad sternly, before we could say anything.

"But the girls would love it," Wes said.

"I don't think it's appropriate for kids," Dad announced.

Dad has brought us up by himself, ever since Mum died. Sometimes I think this makes him take his responsibilities too seriously. (Or maybe he's just too fond of hot baths and a comfortable bed!) Anyway, though I pleaded (and Wild Thing shouted!), he wouldn't change his mind.

Wes tried too. "Oh, go on, Tom. You and the girls would have a great time!"

"Can you imagine Wild Thing at a rock festival?"

"Yeah, but Kate would help keep an eye on her, and Kate's really sensible."

I wasn't pleased. "Actually, I'm not always sensible," I told him. "I can be wild and crazy too."

"All the more reason to stay home, then," said Dad, trying to scrub chocolate sauce off Wild Thing's face.

"But—"

"And you, Kate, should be sensible enough to understand that's final."

Sensible! I was getting sick of hearing that word!

8

Sometimes, things you feel at night vanish by the next morning. Like, for example, when I've squabbled with Bonnie and gone to bed thinking that we'd never, ever be friends again. And the next morning it didn't seem too bad, and by the time we met up at school we'd both more or less forgotten it.

This wasn't one of those times.

I want to be wild, I thought as I crunched my cornflakes. I was trying to crunch them as loudly as possible to drown out the noise of Wild Thing's violin playing from upstairs (Dad was right – it did sound just like a cat being strangled), not to mention Hound Dog howling along with her.

It didn't work.

A few moments later Wild Thing came bounding into the room, waving her violin bow. She almost took out my eye.

"My violin teacher is called Mrs Peters," she announced.

"Oh yeah," I said. "I've seen her around school."

"What's she like?" asked Wild Thing.

"Well . . . she's a bit of an old dinosaur. But she's OK."

Wild Thing looked interested. "What kind of dinosaur?"

"What do you mean?"

"Well, is she a stegosaurus or a pterodactyl?"

"More like a stegosaurus, I'd say. You'll find out."

Then we had to get ready for school. Wild Thing took her violin with her. You wouldn't believe what an effort it was, getting it there. For starters, as we went out of the front door, she dropped it on my toe.

"Ow!" I yelled. The violin travels in a solid case, and it's heavy.

"You don't need to make such a fuss, Kate," Dad told me.

A minute later, as we were going out of the front gate, Wild Thing dropped the violin on *his* toe.

"*OWWWW!*" yelled Dad at the top of his voice. (Plus a few other words that children are always being told they must never, ever say.)

"You don't need to make such a fuss, Dad," I said sweetly.

"Yes I do! I think she's broken it!" Dad hopped about, clutching his foot.

Wild Thing knelt on the ground and opened her violin case. "No, it's not broken."

"I didn't mean your violin, I meant my foot," Dad snapped.

Once Dad had recovered, he tried to get the violin and Wild Thing on to the back of his bike. He often cycles to school, with Wild Thing in a special seat, while I ride my own bike or walk alongside. But there was no way Dad could balance Wild Thing *and* her violin.

"Stupid instrument!" said Dad. "I can manage a full-size guitar, but not this wretched violin." He looked at me. "Kate . . . I wonder . . . could you help us out here?"

I groaned. "Oh, great! So now *I* have to lug her violin!"

"Please, Kate."

So I agreed. I could see that we were going to be late otherwise. But we hadn't reckoned on Wild Thing.

"No!" she shrieked, when I tried to take the handle. "It's mine! *Mine!* You're not having it!"

"But Wild Thing—"

"NO, NO, NO!"

Dad was breathing heavily by now. "OK, let's all walk," he said. "I expect it will be quicker in the end."

Miss Deng gave me a very cross look when I scuttled in late. I soon forgot about Wild Thing's violin though because, sure enough, everyone was busy talking about Wild Thing being a panther. "Poor Kate," Fiona said (in a loud voice so that I was sure to hear), "I do feel *so* sorry for her being stuck with a sister like that!"

Bonnie took my arm and said, "Don't worry, Kate. After all, nobody thinks *you're* like Wild Thing. You're not crazy – you're really sensible!"

"That's the trouble," I muttered. Bonnie looked surprised.

At lunchtime, we had band practice. I love playing in our band. Bonnie's brother Zach started it with some of his friends. Zach and Big Sam play guitar, Little Sam (well, he's little compared to Big Sam) sings, Dylan plays keyboards and Henry is on drums. I play saxophone, and sometimes Bonnie joins us on her tambourine. We all have a great time.

But today, towards the end, Henry lost the rhythm and everyone got in a terrible muddle. After we'd come to a complete halt, Zach said, "Still, *you* were playing the right rhythm, Kate. Completely solid. We can always rely on you."

He was meaning to be nice but . . . solid? It wasn't what I wanted to hear.

After school, I met Wild Thing in the school playground.

"So how was your first violin lesson?" I asked. I was curious, I have to admit.

"Good," Wild Thing told me. "I'm a natural."

Before I could say anything to this, I saw Wild Thing's violin teacher, Mrs Peters, coming towards us. She's very tall with a big, beaky nose and a stern expression.

"*There* you are, Josephine," she said. "You forgot your music book. You won't be able to practise without it, will you?" She held out the book.

"Thank you," said Wild Thing, taking it.

"Now, make sure you practise every day."

"I will."

Mrs Peters turned to go, but before she could, Wild Thing looked at me. "*I* don't think she's an old dinosaur, Kate," she said in a loud voice. "Why did you say she was?"

I felt like the ground was about to swallow me up.

*

I marched home, thinking all the time how mad I was with Wild Thing, and how fed up I was of being Sensible Kate. Wild Thing was chattering away behind me. After a while I began to register what she was saying.

". . .and now I can play the violin, Kate, I can be in a band too. I can be in *your* band. I can play the Wild Thing song!"

I was so horrified by this terrible idea that I stopped short, which meant that Wild Thing cannoned into the back of me.

"Oof!" said Wild Thing. She rubbed her nose. "Why are you standing still, Kate? Are you pretending to be a lamp post?"

As if anyone would pretend to be a lamp post! Though come to think of it, it was just the kind of thing Wild Thing *would* do.

"I suppose *you* think I'm too sensible to pretend to be a lamp post," I told my puzzled sister. "Well, I've got news for you. There's about to be some changes around here!"

I turned and started for home, with a surprised Wild Thing running to catch up. As I went, I couldn't help muttering under my breath.

"Sensible! I've had just about enough of that word."

I reckoned it was time to stop being sensible!

As soon as I got in, I picked up the phone and called Bonnie.

"Listen, Bon, will you come straight round? I need your help. This is an emergency!"

Bonnie turned up ten minutes later with her brother Harris, who was due a guitar lesson with Dad, and while Harris was chatting with Wild Thing about whether bears like eating fish or honey better (Harris and Wild Thing get on really well), Bonnie and I went up to my room. Then all my feelings came pouring out.

"Wild Thing's always getting me into trouble. And sometimes I think she has all the fun. Plus I'm tired of being the sensible one. That's what everyone calls me. And I'm beginning to feel that people think – well – that I'm *boring*."

"You're not boring, Kate," said Bonnie. "I mean, just because you're not completely bonkers like Wild Thing doesn't mean you're boring."

"Are you sure?"

"Course I am! Do you think I'd put up with a boring best friend?"

"No." I smiled. "Thanks. Still – I'd like to do something a bit crazy. A bit unexpected. Take everyone by surprise."

Bonnie's eyes went round as saucers. "Like what?"

"I don't know. That's the trouble."

"Maybe you could go crazy and smash all the computers in the school? Or throw paint at Miss Deng?"

"Are *you* crazy? I don't want them to call the police! And there's no way I'm messing with Miss Deng!" (Miss Deng can be tough. She's fine if you behave yourself, but she's not somebody to cross. There's a rumour in school that she's a black belt in karate.)

I didn't think much of Bonnie's *next* idea either – that I should somehow sneak Hound Dog into school and let him loose during school dinners.

"So what *do* you want to do, Kate?"

"I don't know." I got up and stared at myself in the mirror in my wardrobe door. "I *look* too sensible. I want to look a bit more – wild."

"Maybe you could go to school in a gorilla costume?" Bonnie suggested.

She really didn't get it.

We were still sitting there, trying to think of something, when Wild Thing came bouncing in. She was carrying a large, muddy branch which she dropped on to *my* bed.

"Do you want to see my bear dance? It's where I'm a bear doing a dance in the woods. This is a tree."

"No," I growled. "And get that branch off my bed."

"But I need it. I'm practising for *The Jungle Book*." Wild Thing picked up her branch and began waving it around.

"We're busy on an important mission," Bonnie told her. "We're trying to think of how to make Kate look different. A bit more wild and exciting."

Actually, I'd have preferred for Wild Thing *not* to know this. But it was too late now. She got very excited and dropped her branch (scattering dirt and bark all over my rug). "Oh yes, I'll help!"

Bonnie said to me, "How about piercing your ears?"

"*That's* not wild. Lots of girls at school have pierced ears."

"A pierced *nose!*" yelled Wild Thing. "Like a bull!"

Bonnie snorted with laughter. I wasn't amused. "Nobody would pierce my nose," I told my sister. "Not without Dad's permission."

"*I* would," said Wild Thing. She picked up one of my knitting needles that was lying on the side and started advancing on me.

"Put that down!" I squeaked.

"It won't hurt," said Wild Thing.

"*Of course* it will hurt!" (Like you could stick a knitting needle through someone without it hurting!)

I managed to wrestle the knitting needle away from Wild Thing. Then I put my knitting on a *very* high shelf. I didn't want to wake up one night to find my sister jabbing holes in me.

"Maybe we could do something with your hair," suggested Bonnie.

"She could wear my wig," said Wild Thing at once. "My purple one!"

"It's no good wearing a wig to school," I said. "They'll just make me take it off."

"Hair dye!" declared Bonnie. "They can't make you take that off."

I stared at her. "Hmm . . . maybe . . . I don't know. Anyway, we don't have any hair dye."

"No, but my mum's got loads in the bathroom cabinet," said Bonnie.

I hesitated.

"*I* want hair dye!" declared Wild Thing. "Not Kate! I want my hair in *stripes!*"

That made up my mind. "Well, tough," I told her. "It's not all about you. This time it's about *me*. And it's me that's going to dye my hair, *not* you."

We left a note for Dad and headed over to Bonnie's house.

Bye bye, sensible Kate, I thought.

84

9

For the rest of the afternoon the three of us played hairdressers.

Luckily, Bonnie's mum, Susie, was outside doing some gardening. So we had a clear run at the bathroom, and the boxes of dye in the bathroom cupboard, and all the fluffy, pink bath towels.

"Just lie back and relax!" Bonnie cooed, and that's what I did. It *was* kind of relaxing, until Wild Thing almost yanked a big chunk out of my hair by mistake. But mainly I just lay back and floated away into a dream where I appeared the next day in the classroom and everyone's heads swung round, and they were all like, "Who's *that*?" And somebody said, "Kate," and then they all were like, "Kate, wow, just *look* at her, I'd never have believed it!" Meanwhile I was slinking around the classroom with my new hair, like a funky, cool rock chick. And Fiona was sitting there looking like she'd just swallowed a lemon.

It was great not being sensible, I decided. It was something I was definitely going to do more often.

I was still in this happy-go-lucky mood when Bonnie took off the towel and guided me in front of the long mirror in Susie's bedroom. Bonnie had her hands over my eyes so I couldn't see anything. Wild Thing was there too, chuckling to herself.

"You look great, Kate," she kept saying. "Like a dog's dinner!" (I hoped I *didn't* look like Hound Dog's dinner. But I knew Wild Thing often picked up strange expressions.)

"You look super cool, Kate!" Bonnie assured me.

"I can't wait," I said.

"Ta-da!" said Bonnie. And she took her hands away from my eyes.

There was a long silence.

I stared at myself in the glass.

"Just like a dog's dinner," said Wild Thing again. She was beaming. As if everything was absolutely wonderful.

"Err . . . so what do you think?" asked Bonnie tentatively. Her eyes were not quite meeting mine in the mirror.

I stared at my hair. I hadn't realized how fond of it I was until Bonnie and Wild Thing got at it. I mean, it's just straight, brown, ordinary hair. But now there wasn't any brown to be seen. And they hadn't chosen just *one* colour, as I'd expected. They had done lots of different ones. In *stripes*.

Besides that, some of it was stuck together in clumps, and it had a strange, frizzy look to it, like I was a cartoon character who'd stuck its fingers into an electric socket. Some of it even had *bits* stuck to it. "What were you thinking?" I wailed at them. "I *do* look like a dog's dinner – after he's thrown it up!"

"I wouldn't say that," said Bonnie nervously. I could tell that now she was seeing me in the mirror, she was realizing what a mess she'd made. "I mean, maybe we got a bit carried away, but you did say you wanted to look *wild*."

"You look like a rainbow," Wild Thing said.

"A rainbow! At least a rainbow has proper colours!"

Because my hair was a horrible mixture. Some of it was really strong colours, the kind you'd get from a young child's paint box – bright red and neon pink and lime green. (I couldn't think *where* they'd got them, as I couldn't imagine Bonnie's mum ever wearing them.) But some was a horrible muddy shade, and then there was a hunk of what I can only describe as vomit green.

"And what are the *bits*?"

"The bits?"

"The bits stuck in my hair. The ones that look like cornflakes."

"They look funky," Wild Thing explained.

"Err, Wild Thing put those in," said Bonnie. "And I think . . . they might be. . ."

"What?"

"Hamster food. For Zach's hamsters."

I didn't know what to say.

"You look lovely," Wild Thing told me. "I'd *love* to have hair like that."

I made a kind of growling noise.

"I like playing hairdressers," Wild Thing continued. "It's my new favourite game."

I'd have liked to play hairdressers at that moment. Wild Thing wouldn't have had any hair left by the time I'd finished with her!

Then another thought struck me. "And what will happen tomorrow? I mean, what will they say at *school*?" At the awfulness of this thought, I gave a big sniff and came very close to bursting into tears.

I guess it was good and bad that Bonnie's mum walked in at that moment. Good because I didn't burst into tears. Or start pulling out Wild Thing's hair. Bad because Susie was *furious*. About my hair, but also about the three big, fluffy, pink bath towels that were now covered in dye. Not to mention the bath mat, *and* two face flannels, *and* Bonnie's and mine and Wild Thing's clothes, *and* the drips of dye that went all across the landing and on to her bedroom rug.

On the other hand, it was mainly Bonnie she was mad at. Which wasn't fair really, because Wild Thing and I were just as much to blame. But Wild Thing got away with it because she was little (as usual), and as for me, I think when she saw my hair, not to mention the expression on my face, Susie felt more sorry for me than anything.

"Never mind, Kate," she said when she'd finished scolding Bonnie. "I'm sure that some of those colours will wash out and . . . well, hair *grows*, doesn't it? But I don't know what your dad will say."

We found out soon enough, when Dad turned up wanting to go to the supermarket and to take Wild Thing and me with him. Being Dad, he wasn't that upset about my hair. He just said, "Oh, Kate!" and started to laugh.

"It's not funny," I said fiercely.

"Well – it is a bit," he said.

"It's a *disaster*," I told him. "A catastrophe! The

end of the world! No *way* am I going to school like this! In fact, I'm not even going outside the house until it's all grown out."

But then Dad turned really hard-hearted. He said no way was I staying off school. I'd always thought Dad was pretty understanding, as parents go, so I was really shocked at his cruel attitude.

"But I just *can't* let people see me like this," I moaned. "It's too humiliating!" But Dad was immovable. Wild Thing offered to dye her hair to match, to make me feel better. I said *nothing* was *ever* going to make me feel better.

Susie was great, though. She sent Dad and Wild Thing off to the supermarket. Then she washed my hair herself, using some special hair rinse. Some of the colours did come out: it turned out that the really bright ones were spray-on colours left over from Halloween, and they weren't permanent. Some of the clumpiness came out too. And all of the hamster food.

But some of the colours didn't. After Susie

had rinsed my hair three times, most of it was looking more or less brown, but I was left with a big purplish-coloured stripe of hair right down the middle of my head!

"It looks lots better, Kate, really," Susie told me.

"Honest, it does," Bonnie promised.

"I think it's going to be a great look when you play with the band," said Zach, who had just got back from the skateboard park.

It was all very well for them – I was wondering what Fiona would say at school the next morning!

10

I guess Wild Thing wouldn't have thought twice about swanning into school with purple hair, but I felt like curling up somewhere to hide. Dad, to my surprise, gave my hand a big squeeze before I stepped through the gates that morning. "Smile, Kate," he said. "And walk in there with your head held high!"

So I did my best. Although it wasn't that easy when all the boys were laughing and pointing, and all the girls were staring. I definitely heard Fiona whisper to her friends, "She's going to be in so much trouble now!"

But to my surprise, apart from a raised eyebrow, Miss Deng didn't say anything. And my own friends, like Livy and Jemima, said they reckoned I looked great! Still, I hated having everybody staring at me, and it was actually quite a relief when by lunchtime suddenly everybody was talking about Wild Thing instead.

Apparently she had built one of her dens in the Little Ones' playground, and it had collapsed on Miss Randolph's head. (Miss Randolph is the Little Ones' teacher.) Luckily it was only made of cardboard and clothes from the Little Ones' dressing-up box, although Miss Randolph did have to go to the school nurse, and she ended up with a sticking plaster on her nose. (*I* couldn't help thinking it was Miss Randolph's fault for crawling in there in the first place. I mean, just because Wild Thing had invited her in for a "bear breakfast" of honey and berries didn't mean she had to say yes.)

Then, when Wild Thing was collecting her plate of sausage and mash for lunch, she had growled at the dinner ladies, and even snapped her teeth at one, who was so surprised she dropped a whole pan of mashed potato. *That* caused a sensation.

"Hey, that Josephine is wild!"

"She keeps you entertained, doesn't she?"

"What does she think she is – a crocodile?"

So what with that, and band practice, and the maths test Miss Deng sprang on us, I had almost forgotten about my hair until the very end of the afternoon when Miss Deng said, "Come here a moment, Kate."

I went to stand by her desk, feeling sure that I was about to be told off. I think a lot of the other kids thought the same, because several of them lingered, hoping to overhear, until Miss Deng gave them a stern look and they scuttled out to the cloakroom.

"I see you've been experimenting with hair dye," said Miss Deng, when the classroom was empty.

"Yes – and I really wish I hadn't," I said feelingly. "I'm not doing it again!"

"That's good," said Miss Deng. "Because I'm sure you know that coloured hair is *not* part of the school dress code."

"I know – I'm sorry."

"Don't worry about it too much, Kate," said Miss Deng, smiling. "We all have experiments that go wrong. I remember, when I was just a bit older than you, I coloured *my* hair. Because it's so dark, I had to use peroxide first, and then I tried to turn it red – a lovely, deep, chestnut red it looked on the packet, but. . ." She made a face.

"What happened?"

"It went pink. Salmon pink."

"Eek!"

"Yes. *Much* worse than a purple stripe. Actually," Miss Deng said thoughtfully, "I think your stripe looks rather nice."

Dad came to meet me and Wild Thing from school. He listened patiently as Wild Thing told him the exciting story of how her den fell on top of Miss Randolph. "Stupid old bison," was how Wild Thing put it. "She shouldn't have such a big bottom."

"Wild Thing!" I hissed. "You mustn't say things about teachers' bottoms! Anyway, Miss Randolph's bottom is quite small, for a grown-up's."

"It's too big for my den," said Wild Thing. "That's the bit that got stuck. And then she wiggled it about and everything fell down. I spent ages building that den!"

Dad managed to stop laughing at last, and told Wild Thing not to call her teacher a bison. Also, he said that she mustn't growl at the dinner ladies (the school had phoned him up at home to complain). Then he said he was taking us to a coffee shop. "It's a treat for Kate, really. Because she's had a tough few days."

Thankfully milkshake with chocolate marshmallows was enough to take Wild Thing's mind off Miss Randolph. Then, when she went to the toilet, Dad asked me, "So how *was* school today?"

"It was OK," I said. "Actually, it wasn't as bad as I expected."

"Good," said Dad. He stirred his coffee. "Kate, was there any particular reason you decided to colour your hair?"

I stared hard at my empty plate. Then I started to explain, but it all came out a bit smothered: "Wild Thing ... all the attention ... everyone thinks she's special ... stupid olives ... stupid violin ... nobody notices me ... Fiona ... sensible ... tired of it ... seemed like a good idea at the time."

Dad put his arm round my shoulders. "You know, Kate, you don't have to act like Wild Thing. You're wonderful as you are. You're musical ... you sing and play *really* well ... you have lots of friends because you're fun and you're kind. I know it sounds corny and a bit of a cliché ... but all you need to be is you."

I gave a huge sniff. "I know."

"Good ... because to be honest, I don't think I could handle it if you turned into another Wild Thing."

It was at this point Wild Thing came back. She'd managed to tuck the toilet paper into the

99

back of her pants by mistake so that when she came skipping between the tables, a long trail of pink paper came after her. After we'd managed to unwind her, Dad made us sit down again and said he had something to tell us.

"What is it?" we demanded.

"I've been thinking you both deserve some kind of treat. Well, actually, you *don't* deserve a treat, Wild Thing, but Kate does. She's had to put up with a lot, what with that birthday party, and then there's the matter of her hair. . ."

"*I* deserve a treat too," said Wild Thing.

"You don't, but at least it might stop you building dens in Kate's bedroom. I was remembering how much you both wanted to go camping. . ." And then Dad said he'd been talking some more to Wes about the rock festival that was taking place at half-term at Brammingham, and what a great place it was, and such a lovely campsite, and how very suitable for kids. And it would be a chance for Dad to play with the band again. So he had decided to take us.

"Yay!" we both yelled together. "We're going camping!"

We started packing as soon as we got home.

MY PACKING

Waterproof jacket and trousers
Wellington boots
Lots of woolly socks

Toothbrush and toothpaste
Dustbin bags (to keep everything dry)
A torch
A head torch that you attach to your head (in case
you need the toilet in the night)
Toilet paper (in case the campsite toilets ran out)
A picnic rug
A thermos flask

WILD THING'S PACKING

Purple rock-star wig
A jam jar full of worms
Robin Hood bow-and-arrow set
A pirate fancy-dress costume
Six more jam jars (for collecting worms)
A book called *Bears and Their Habitats*
One of Gran's old handbags labelled "WORM
HOUSE - KEEP OUT"
A violin.

Dad didn't seem too worried about what we packed, except that, to my surprise, he said we should take my guitar. "But I won't have time to play it," I pointed out. Dad just looked vague and said to bring it anyway.

The next day I told Bonnie and Zach about our trip. They were really excited. "Maybe *we* can all come too," said Bonnie.

"Yeah!" Zach could hardly keep still. "After all, if your dad thinks it's OK then maybe Mum will, too."

"Err, yes," I said.

I guess I didn't sound too keen because Bonnie said crossly, what was the matter, didn't I *want* them to come? And I said of *course* I did, what was she on about? Actually, the truth is that I *wasn't* keen, not because I didn't want them to come but because I'd been counting on us borrowing their tent!

So I spent the rest of the day on tenterhooks, worrying, while Wild Thing was crashing around the house. When I finally paid attention I found she'd tied a backpack on to poor Hound Dog, only it was too loose and had slipped round under his tummy. "He's got to pack his things," Wild Thing explained. "He's got a pig's ear, his blanket, his favourite doggy chews, a torch in case he's scared of the dark. . ." While we were arguing about this (I didn't see how he could possibly work a torch, but Wild Thing claimed he could push the buttons with his nose), Bonnie phoned. She said Susie had decided that they *could* go, and I had to pretend to be really pleased. I spent another nail-biting half hour wondering what we would do for a tent, before Dad remarked quite casually that Max's family had said we could borrow *their* tent. So that was all right.

It turned out Max's tent was even fancier than Bonnie's, with a canopy over the entrance and three bedrooms. Wild Thing reckoned it would be as good as Buckingham Palace!

By now, we could hardly wait.

11

On the day before half-term, the Little Ones did their performance of *The Jungle Book*. Only grown-up family were invited, so I was saved the embarrassment of watching Wild Thing (dressed as Bagheera the Panther) turn to the audience and shout at the top of her voice, "She's not really a bear! It's just a bear costume. She's really a snake! Look!" and then try to pull Nerisa's bear head off. At which point Nerisa lost her temper completely and yelled, "I *am* a bear, I'm a wonderful bear, you stupid old panther! And leave my head alone!" Then they began pushing and shoving each other, and growling and biting like a pair of real bears, until both of them went rolling off the stage into the wings.

"Absolutely disgraceful," said Gran afterwards. "I've never seen anything like it."

"Yes," agreed Dad. "Best school play I've seen in years."

Gran told Dad off for this, but he said he was sure most of the audience agreed with him. "Max's dad fell off his chair, he was laughing so much!"

I almost wished I'd seen the play myself.

Still – "Tomorrow we're really heading for the woods!" I declared. Everyone agreed with that, and Wild Thing began bouncing around explaining how she was going to be Queen of the Jungle. Gran made pizza for us while we finished some last-minute packing. There was a horrible moment when we thought everything wasn't going to fit in the car – but it did. Just. Then we wolfed down the pizza while Gran gave us various tips about using mosquito repellent, and keeping Wild Thing away from ponds, and not tripping over the guy rope, but I hardly listened I was so excited.

It took *ages* to get to sleep. I kept thinking of extra things I might need and getting up to find them. While I was searching for my old butterfly net, I heard a *thump* from Wild Thing's room and went in to find her staring at a lamp, which was in pieces on the floor. "What's going on?" I asked.

"I got it with my lasso."

"What lasso?"

"*This* lasso." She waved the lasso from her cowboy set. "I'm taking it camping. It will be very useful."

"Useful for what?" I asked.

"For lassoing things, of course." Wild Thing shook her head at my stupidity.

I was far too tired to argue with her, and went back to bed.

The next morning we were up before seven. We took Hound Dog for a quick run, then we left our house keys with Mrs Crabbe next door and we all piled into the car. Gran arrived just in time to wave us goodbye.

"Really, I'm quite jealous," she told us. "I used to go camping with the Girl Guides when I was young."

"You can come if you like," said Dad. "I mean, we'll make space somehow." He glanced doubtfully at the pile of jackets and sleeping bags and my guitar case that were all wedged into the front seat.

"No, no," said Gran. "I'm not sleeping in a tent at my age." She was smiling in a rather mysterious way. "Have a wonderful time. I'll see you when I see you!" And she stood waving as we pulled out of the drive.

Ten minutes. A mere ten minutes. That was how long it took before our first stop. The reason? Wild Thing needed the toilet.

Twenty minutes later she said she needed to go again.

Ten minutes after *that* Wild Thing and me asked Dad if we could stop for Hound Dog – he kept whining. Dad said absolutely not. And about a minute later Hound Dog threw up – all over me *and* Wild Thing *and* Dad's jacket *and* everything else on the back seat.

So then we had to stop to clean up.

"Wretched dog," muttered Dad.

"It's not his fault he's carsick," said Wild Thing.

Eventually we set off again with Hound Dog wagging his tail cheerfully, and five minutes later Wild Thing asked, "Are we nearly there yet?"

We hadn't even joined the motorway.

Dad groaned.

Eventually we came off the motorway again, and the roads got smaller and smaller, until finally they were just winding lanes with high hedges on either side. Every time we went past a gate I could see green fields, with cows or sheep grazing. I began to feel really excited (almost as excited as Hound Dog, who kept barking at the sheep). Wild Thing was fast asleep by now, so (apart from Hound Dog barking) it felt lovely and peaceful.

The only problem was that there weren't many signposts. And Dad didn't seem too sure where we were going. "This lane wasn't supposed to be here," he muttered as we arrived at a crossroads.

"I thought Wes gave you directions?" I said.

"He did," Dad replied, "but . . . well . . . you see, I've been here before and I was sure I remembered the way so . . . I didn't pay much attention." He hadn't bothered to write down Wes's directions either. And when he got out his phone to try and find a map, it turned out we were so deep in the country that it didn't have any reception.

"I'm beginning to think we might need to stop and ask somebody," said Dad, "if only there were anyone to ask."

"No, we don't – just turn right!" I yelled.

"Great – did you spot a sign?"

"No, but I just saw Bonnie's van going that way, so now all we need to do is follow them!"

Luckily Susie is very organized. She doesn't travel anywhere without a road atlas, a satnav, a mobile phone and detailed instructions printed off the Internet. We just kept right behind her, and in no time at all we were turning into the drive of a very grand house, and then following the signs that led to the campsite.

Dad had said it was quite a small festival but it felt like there were loads of people there. In the distance, I could see the big tents and stages where the bands would play. Here on the campsite there seemed to be lots of people milling around, parking cars, setting up tents or just lying out on the grass sunning themselves. We reached the wooded end of the field and Susie parked under an enormous oak tree, while we stopped a little further on, near a stream.

"Perfect," said Dad, very pleased with himself. "I'm surprised nobody else has taken this good spot."

Wild Thing woke up then, and was very excited. "Want to explore!"

So we did. The stream was one of those lovely burbling ones, the kind people write poems about, with crystal-clear water running over flat, smooth pebbles. It was perfect for paddling but also (as Dad pointed out) not deep enough for Wild Thing to drown herself. Next to the stream were wild flowers, and pretty bushes rather than prickly ones, and a big, level stretch of grass, just right for our tent. And beyond that were the woods: they weren't gloomy, dark woods either, but full of beech trees with fresh green leaves and bluebells growing in between.

"I'm going deep into the jungle!" cried Wild Thing, as Hound Dog set off in pursuit of a rabbit. And she charged after him.

Soon Bonnie and Zach turned up. They were just as excited as I was, and reckoned this was one of the best camping places they'd been to. We decided to follow the stream. We soon came across Wild Thing (who was crashing about the undergrowth like a herd of elephants). "I've found a crocodile lagoon," she told us, and led us to a place where the stream widened out into a little pool. Somebody had tied a rope to the branch of a tree so that you could swing out over the water. "Me first!" yelled Wild Thing. "I'm the Jungle Queen!"

We all took turns, until it was Wild Thing's go again. "I'm Wild Thing, Queen of the Jungle!" she yelled as she jumped off the bank. Only this time she was only holding on to the rope with one hand, so that she could beat her chest with her fist and make Tarzan noises.

"I don't think that's very –"

SPLASH!

"– safe," I finished, as Wild Thing fell in with a shower of spray.

By the time we'd pulled her out (Wild Thing insisted that she'd only escaped the crocodiles by inches) we were all sodden. We squelched back to find out how Dad was doing with the tent.

Not too well, it turned out. I'd been there when Max's dad explained *exactly* how to put it up, and I suppose I should have been able to tell from the expression on Dad's face as he said "Yeah – yeah – right you are" every now and then that he wasn't taking it in.

"You see, the thing is, I *know* how to put up a tent," Dad explained, when I asked him why he hadn't listened more carefully. "I've done it loads of times."

"Then what's going wrong?"

"I'm not sure. Maybe they didn't give us all the bits. . . I can't work it out."

Zach, Bonnie, Wild Thing and I decided to "help", but although we enjoyed ourselves, the tent didn't seem any further on than before. Dad was getting a bit short-tempered too. I was beginning to think we'd have to follow Wild Thing's suggestion and build a den in the woods when Susie and Harris turned up. They had just finished putting up their own tent, and it didn't take them more than a few moments to work out how to put up ours (once they had found out where Wild Thing had hidden the pegs and stopped Hound Dog playing tug of war with the poles).

Our tent was enormous! Wild Thing and I ran inside to inspect it and argue about bedrooms while Hound Dog ran in and out, barking. Then Dad said, "Right, time for some grub!"

Susie said she would take the dogs for a walk in the woods, and the rest of us set off for the main festival. That's when I made the wonderful discovery that festivals aren't just about music, they're about *food* too. There were loads of food stalls, and we spent ages choosing, then pigging out on wraps and hot dogs and fritters and ice cream. (Wild Thing drove Dad crazy because she couldn't decide what to have, and ended up eating a bit of everything.)

Afterwards we all felt very full, so it was good to flop down on the grass and watch a bunch of jugglers and unicyclists doing their stuff.

"Wow," I said to Bonnie and Zach. "Camping is even better than I thought."

Zach didn't reply. Instead he sat up and pointed into the crowd.

"What's Wild Thing up to now?" he asked.

12

Wild Thing had decided to join the jugglers. To be fair, they were inviting people from the crowd to join in. Still, I watched rather nervously as she picked up two of the batons and chucked them in the air.

"Hey, she's good," said Zach. She was. She was juggling two batons like she'd been doing it all her life.

"Good job, Wild Thing!" we called.

Wild Thing smirked at us. One of the jugglers said, "Hey, you're doing really well with two – want to have a go with three?"

"Yes," said Wild Thing.

"I'll just show you how it's done."

"No need," said Wild Thing loftily. She grabbed the third baton, then threw each of them, one by one, into the air.

Up went the first baton.

Up went the second baton.

The third baton flew sideways and bonked the juggler on the nose.

"Ow!" he said.

Wild Thing got cross. "Stupid, stupid juggling!" She threw the batons on the ground. Dad rushed out onto the grass, grabbed hold of Wild Thing and apologized to the juggler.

"But juggling *is* stupid!" she yelled as he marched her away.

Soon after this, Dad bumped into some musician friends of his. They started chatting, which was a bit boring for us kids, so after a while Dad said we could go and explore, just so long as Harris went too.

We could see the big house in the distance, so we went to check it out. As we drew closer, we discovered it was enormous, the kind of place dukes and duchesses lived in, years ago. Bonnie wanted to explore the gardens, but I said, "Where's Wild Thing?"

"Isn't she with Harris?" asked Zach. We went over to Harris, who was watching some African drumming, but he said he'd assumed Wild Thing was with us.

"Oh, great!" I declared. "She's lost!"

"There's probably a meeting point for lost children," said Bonnie. "There always is at big events."

"You obviously don't know Wild Thing very well," I replied. "The last thing she would ever do is to go to a meeting point for lost children. That would be far too sensible."

"Well, let's split up and search for her then," said Zach.

So we did. We couldn't find her anywhere. It was while we were standing near the drive to the big house, wondering what on earth to do next, that she suddenly popped out from behind an enormous stone lion.

"Boo!"

"Argh!" I shrieked. "Wild Thing! Where have you been?"

"Yes, we've been looking everywhere," Bonnie told her.

"Oh. I wondered what you were looking for."

I could have killed my sister! "Why didn't you come and tell us you were there?"

"Because I was playing spies. And spies are *secret*."

I looked at Harris. After all, he was the oldest. "Why don't you tell her off?" But Harris just thinks Wild Thing is funny.

"Who were you spying on?" he asked. "Bad guys in disguise?"

"Maybe. I found someone who looks just like Gran."

I snorted. "There is nobody at this festival who looks like Gran!"

"Yes, there is. I think they're *personating* her."

I pointed out that nobody would want to impersonate Gran. Even if somebody did want to disguise themselves for some reason, Gran would be the last person to choose. She was way older than most people at the festival, and wearing the wrong clothes.

"You're wrong," said Wild Thing. "Look!"

She grabbed hold of my arm and we all looked in the direction she was pointing.

A big camper van was parked in front of the fountain near the house. An older lady leaned against the door of the van, talking into her mobile phone. Apart from the fact she was about Gran's age, she looked nothing like her.

I pointed this out. "Though maybe she's the owner of the house," I added, eyeing her beautifully styled silver hair, elegant tweed jacket and high-heeled shoes.

"Not *her*!" said Wild Thing. "Her!" And then I saw that there was another lady, round near the front of the camper van, talking to a security guard. She had brown hair, a sensible fleece, blue hiking trousers and lace-up shoes.

"Actually, she does look quite like Gran," I said. "Her jacket is just the same. . ." And that's when I realized the truth. It looked like Gran because . . . it *was* Gran!

We all went racing over. Gran gave Wild Thing and me a hug. She was smiling broadly – you could tell she was really pleased with herself for giving us such a surprise.

"But what are you DOING here?" we demanded, and Gran explained that her friend Julia had been coming down, and had invited Gran to come too.

"And she has this lovely camper van, *so* comfortable, all mod cons. Hot and cold water, a shower, a wonderful fitted kitchen and a table for us to play cards of an evening. We'll be able to cook all kinds of things, and I must show you the kettle—"

Gran seemed like she could go on about the camper van and its amazing amenities for ever, but Wild Thing, rather rudely, interrupted her.

"But WHY are you here? Or her? You're too *old*." Which wasn't very polite, but it was true. (I mean, Gran's not *that* old. But she was a lot older than most of the music fans at the festival.)

Luckily Gran was in too good a mood to be annoyed by Wild Thing, and she explained that Julia was friends with the owners of the big house. Then Gran added casually, almost as an afterthought, "And, of course, she knew that her granddaughters were going to be here."

I felt as if the blood ran cold in my veins. "Her granddaughters?"

"Yes," said Gran. "Dear Fiona and Nerisa are here too."

I gave a screech and so did Wild Thing. I guess neither of us were thrilled with this piece of news!

"But *why* are they here?" asked Bonnie. "It's just not their thing."

"I think Julia said something about a new girl band that they like."

Bonnie and I looked at each other and pulled faces. "Oh well," muttered Bonnie. "At least we know now to avoid her."

Wild Thing was more forthright. "I hate that Nissa," she announced. "She's a snake. So there!"

It was bad luck that at the very same moment Wild Thing said this, Nerisa and Fiona's grandmother joined us. Still, I think Gran smoothed things over quite well, all things considered.

Then Dad came looking for us. He was pretty surprised to see Gran, and I'm not sure he was that pleased, especially when she started telling him off for letting us go roaming about without him!

"We ought to be getting back to the campsite," he said.

"Yes," said Wild Thing. "There's something Very Important we need to do."

13

When we got back, Dad announced that he was going to enjoy the sunshine. "I heard there was rain forecast, but just look at these clear skies – what nonsense!" He flung himself out on the grass to sunbathe.

Wild Thing disappeared into the tent. When she poked her head out of the flap a few minutes later, she gave me quite a turn. For a moment I thought it really *was* a bear staring at me: a brown, furry bear with lovely round bear ears. "What *are* you wearing?"

"It's my bear costume. For Baloo."

"But you weren't Baloo, you were Bagheera. Do you mean. . ."

Wild Thing scowled. "I *should* have been Baloo. I *wanted* to be Baloo. I'm a much better

Baloo than that Nissa—"

"But Wild Thing, you can't steal costumes from school—"

Wild Thing ignored me. "Let's go find a bear!"

The rest of us looked at one another. We knew perfectly well there were no bears. On the other hand, it was going to be hard work convincing Wild Thing of that.

"Come on!" Wild Thing called.

"It might be fun," Zach pointed out. Bonnie and I nodded. So we set off, with Wild Thing leading the way.

"Bear alert!" Wild Thing yelled every time she heard a rustle in the undergrowth. Then she would go racing on ahead, only to find a terrier dog snuffling in the bushes or a squirrel running up a tree.

Wild Thing wouldn't believe there were no bears, though. "Look at this!" she would yell, popping up unexpectedly out of the undergrowth. "It's a bear paw print."

"It looks more like a dog print to me," said

Bonnie. "A small dog." But Wild Thing had already raced away in search of more tracks.

Eventually we headed back towards the tents, Wild Thing insisting in a loud voice that it was our fault we hadn't found any bears: we'd been too noisy and frightened them away.

"What cheek!" I declared. "You're noisier than anyone!"

Halfway back to the tents, Wild Thing stopped short. I almost walked into her.

"What is it?" I asked. "Spotted a grizzly?"

"Look where Hound Dog's gone. *That's* where I'm going to build my den!"

I followed her into a clearing. There were tree stumps, a boulder, a glade of grass . . . and a hollow tree. Wild Thing was right. It would be a perfect place to build a den and hide out in the woods.

"Look!" I pointed to a circle of toadstools. "It's a fairy ring."

Wild Thing asked what did that mean, and I explained that the toadstools made a perfect little circle of stools for fairies to sit on when they came out by moonlight. Wild Thing gave me a withering look.

"Don't you know, Kate, there are no such things as fairies?"

This from my sister, who still believes in monsters under the bed, and who was convinced she was going to meet a wild bear any moment.

"What are you up to?" It was Zach and Bonnie.

"Look, we're going to build a den!" Wild Thing showed them the hollow tree. Zach immediately got excited. Bonnie wrinkled her nose.

"Dens are for babies!"

"So you don't have to get involved," Zach told her. Then he turned to Wild Thing and me. "What if we bring over some branches? We can prop them up against the trunk and make an extra room."

While we set to work, Bonnie sat down on a stone with her arms crossed and her nose in the air.

For five minutes she ignored us.

129

For another five, she kept secretly glancing over, trying to see what we were up to.

And five minutes after that, she came rushing over yelling, "Don't do it *that* way! Do it *this* way!"

After that, we heard no more about "babyish". In fact, Bonnie was keener on the den than anybody.

It really was fantastic. We used sturdy branches to make one wall, and Wild Thing gathered moss and put it on top of the branches, so that no rain would be able to come in through the gaps. We tried weaving the willow into screens, although it wasn't as easy as it had looked the time I'd seen it on TV. We had lots more plans too: Bonnie was going to gather stones from the stream to make a path, and I reckoned I could weave a doormat out of rushes, and Wild Thing was planning a special place for her worms, and Zach reckoned if he could get some rope from the campsite then he could make a hammock.

We were all busy and happy, when suddenly

we were brought back to cold reality with a thump.

"*Yoo-hoo!* Kate! Bonnie! It's Fiona!"

Bonnie and I stared at each other. I reckon I felt about as dismayed as Bonnie looked. "Let's hide!"

"Hide? Why?" asked Zach.

"Because this is *our* den and they'll spoil it!"

"But—"

"Oh, stop arguing," said Bonnie. "We know Fiona and you don't. Let's get under cover!"

Bonnie and I hustled Zach into the den. I grabbed Hound Dog by his collar and dragged him in too.

"Where's Wild Thing?" asked Zach.

There was no sign of her. "I think she went to fetch her worms," whispered Bonnie. I just hoped she would have the sense to keep out of sight. After all, she didn't like Fiona and Nerisa either.

Everything went quiet. Then we heard footsteps. We peered through the gaps in the branches and saw Fiona appear on the grass in front of our den. Nerisa was with her. They stood there looking around them. Looking for *us*.

"*I* think they're hiding," said Nerisa.

Know-it-all!

"I think so too," said Fiona. She raised her voice. "You're a bit old for hide-and-seek, Kate! Your dad said you're in the woods, and we're going to find you!"

"Nosy parker," muttered Bonnie.

We were all crammed together. My elbow was digging into Zach's stomach, and I could see a branch sticking into Bonnie's neck, and Bonnie's hair was tickling my nose, and Hound Dog was sitting on our feet, and we were all just about as squashed and uncomfortable as could be. But none of us kids made a sound.

We were as invisible and silent as the best spies. . .

. . .until Hound Dog lifted his head and howled!

"Shh!" we hissed, but Hound Dog wouldn't. And when we tried to grab him and hold his snout shut, he wriggled out of our grasp, zoomed out of the den and went bouncing all over Fiona and Nerisa.

"Get him *off*!" screeched Fiona. "He's muddy!" And sure enough, there were now two enormous paw prints on her white leggings.

"He's just being friendly," said Zach, following me out of the den.

"And white leggings are stupid things to wear camping," Bonnie pointed out. "I mean, what did you expect?"

"We're not *camping*," said Fiona furiously, scrubbing at her leggings. "Mum says she'd die rather than camp out in a muddy field. We're staying in a hotel. We have an en-suite bathroom and everything."

"That sounds no fun to me," I said. I managed to seize Hound Dog's collar just before he could bounce at Nerisa again, and probably send her into the stream.

"It's better than playing stupid, babyish dens!" Fiona snapped.

"Well, why don't you go and do something else then?"

But they didn't move, and I could tell they were just going to stay put and make sure they spoiled all our fun.

Only there was something I'd forgotten.

There was a whistling sound, and before I could even begin to work out what it was – POW! Something hit Fiona right on the bum.

It was an arrow. It bounced off and fell on to the grass.

"Not babyish!" said a voice from behind us. We turned to see Wild Thing peering around the trunk of a tree, her bow in her hands. She had leaves sticking out of her hair – I guess she was trying to disguise herself as a tree.

"Good shot!" said Zach. "Right on the bullseye!"

"You mean the bull's *bum*," said Bonnie, and started giggling.

Wild Thing's bow and arrows are only toys from her Robin Hood set, but you'd think from the fuss Fiona made that Wild Thing had skewered her with a six-foot spear.

"Ow – ow – ow!" she shrieked, clutching her bum with both hands.

"Come off it. It can't have hurt that much," Bonnie said.

"I have very sensitive skin!" Fiona yelled.

I couldn't help giggling; Fiona was so furious.

"Wait until I tell my mum on you!" Fiona

grabbed Nerisa and they stalked off back towards the campsite.

I suppose we should have told Wild Thing off for shooting at people. But we didn't. We were too grateful!

"How did you learn to shoot so well?" asked Zach.

I was wondering the same thing. I was imagining Wild Thing winning gold for archery at the next Olympics. My sister, the medal winner! It turned out, though, that Wild Thing wasn't that great a shot. Her first four arrows had all ended up in the bushes. It was only the fifth that had struck home. Besides, she hadn't actually been aiming at Fiona, she explained – she'd been trying to hit *Nerisa*.

That night, I was so exhausted that even Wild Thing squirming around in her sleeping bag like a giant worm, hissing "that was definitely a bear making that sound – can't *you* hear it, Kate – *definitely* a bear" while Hound Dog turned round and round on my ankles, trying to make himself comfortable, couldn't keep me awake. And besides, whatever Dad had said about rocks in backs when he'd been trying to put us off camping, my mattress was actually very soft.

When I woke up again, it was dark, and I must have been really heavily asleep, because I felt like my arms and legs were tree trunks and I was swimming to the surface of a great pool of treacle. "Go 'way . . . there isn't a bear. . ." I muttered. "No bears at all."

"Wake up, Kate," said Wild Thing in my ear.

With a huge effort, I opened my eyes. "There are NO bears!" I said in a loud voice.

"No bears," said my sister, "but there *is* a flood."

"Huh?"

I struggled to sit up. It's not an easy thing to do in a sleeping bag: your arms get trapped in next to you, and then the sleeping bag gets all twisted round you as you sleep, and the next thing you know – you're stuck.

Not only that, but my sleeping bag felt extremely heavy. Much heavier than when I went to sleep. And then I'd had a dog sitting on me too.

I was also aware of a noise that hadn't been there earlier. It was a very loud drumming sound. Maybe it was from the festival, I thought vaguely, though it sounded awfully close.

"What have you done now?" I demanded.

Just then the flap of the tent opened and Dad stuck his head through. A very wet Hound Dog squeezed past him and flung himself on top of me. As I struggled with sopping-wet dog, I suddenly realized that the drumming noise wasn't somebody playing a drum – it was rain thumping down on the roof of the tent.

At roughly the same time, I noticed what I would have noticed before if I hadn't been half asleep – that it wasn't just Hound Dog who was sopping wet. Water was seeping in through my sleeping bag and I was soaking. "Right, girls," said Dad, "you've got to get up straight away. We've got to move the tent!"

"Move the tent?" I repeated. "Why? What good will that do?"

"We need to move the tent," said Dad, "because at the moment it's in the middle of a river."

It was true. When I finally managed to crawl out of my sleeping bag, and Wild Thing and I had found our wellingtons and waterproof ponchos and stumbled out into the rain, we discovered two things. First, the lovely little stream that we had been camping next to was now a great big river. And second, most of it was swooshing through our tent.

"Flood alert! Flood alert!" yelled Wild Thing, jumping up and down. "Call the fire brigade!"

"Don't be daft," I said. "What are the fire brigade going to do?"

"It's just like Noah's Ark," said Wild Thing. She began to sing. *The animals went in two by two, hurrah, hurrah. . ."*

Dad was desperately trying to get the tent down. I ran to help him. It had been hard enough to get the tent *up* when the weather was dry and sunny. Now, in the darkness, with water churning round our ankles and the rain buffeting down on us, it was almost impossible. "Get our stuff out and on to dry land!" Dad shouted, so I did my best while he wrestled with poles and flapping ground sheets.

"Where's Wild Thing?" asked Dad suddenly.

We looked around. There was no sign of her. "She's probably gone hunting for bears," I said. Then I had a thought. *What if she's been washed away?*

I think Dad was thinking the same thing, because he dropped the tent and went wading into the water, yelling, "Wild Thing! Where are you?" There was a real note of panic in his voice.

It was very dark – even the moon was half-covered by clouds – and it was pretty spooky looking at all that water. I didn't *really* think it was deep enough or strong enough to carry anyone away. But still, I imagined Wild Thing floating along like a piece of driftwood. I imagined a whale swallowing her, or a shark nibbling at her. I've always said I'd love to get rid of my little sister. Now I wasn't so sure.

Then a voice called out, "Here I am!"

It was Wild Thing. Before I could work out if I was pleased or disappointed to see her again, she said, "Look! I couldn't find any firemen. So they'll have to do."

She had brought Bonnie and her family, all of them dressed in waterproof boots and jackets. I decided I *was* pleased to see Wild Thing after all. Susie and Harris went wading out to help Dad with the tent, while Zach and Bonnie helped me to lug the backpacks and sleeping bags and all the other stuff to dry land. (The dogs and Wild Thing didn't help anyone, but splashed cheerfully about in the water.)

We all went back to Susie's tent, which was dry as a bone, and found towels and dry clothes for everyone. And once I had on Bonnie's spare pair of fleecy pyjamas, Harris's hoody and two pairs of Zach's woolly socks, I stopped shivering. As soon as it stopped raining, Susie lit the camping stove and hung up all our wet clothes on a line between two trees. She even towelled down the dogs. Then she made a big pan of hot, sweet, milky cocoa, and we all sat round drinking it. I don't think I've ever tasted anything so delicious in my whole life.

As she poured out seconds of cocoa, she said, "I did wonder why you chose a spot *quite* so close to the stream."

Dad went rather red. "And I was wondering why nobody else had taken it!"

15

When I woke up again, late the following morning, there was no sign of rain. I crawled out into the sunlight, yawning, and glad to stretch myself after a night spent crammed in next to Wild Thing, Bonnie and Zach. It seemed like I'd spent most of the time listening to Zach snoring, or else waking up when somebody's knees and elbows clonked me on the nose!

We all sat out on the grass to eat breakfast (just being a bit careful to avoid the muddy patches). Susie made everyone porridge over the camp stove. Wild Thing complained she didn't like porridge, until somebody pointed out that the Three Bears ate porridge for *their* breakfast, and then she ate three helpings.

"I'm going to make a bear trap," she said with

her mouth full. "I'm going to dig a big pit and put some porridge at the bottom."

"You do that," I said. I added in a low voice to Bonnie, "At least it will keep her out of trouble."

Bonnie winked. "And with any luck, Fiona might come along and fall in it." We both giggled.

Then Gran turned up. She tutted away like anything when she saw where we had pitched our tent. "If only your father had stayed in the Boy Scouts when he was a teenager instead of joining that rock band, then he would have known never to choose a place like that. It's a good thing you weren't all washed away."

"I'd *like* to be washed away," said Wild Thing. "I'd like to be a pirate."

Gran just snorted. Then she took Wild Thing and me off to have showers in her camper van. I must admit, it felt good. I'd never appreciated before what a wonderful invention a hot shower is.

Later, as we walked around the festival with Dad, I couldn't help noticing the way people looked at him, and nudged each other as he went past. Some of them told him they couldn't wait to listen to Monkey Magic, who were going to be performing that afternoon.

I whispered to Zach, who was walking beside me. "Do you see the way people look at Dad? It's like he's . . . famous or something."

"He *is* famous," said Zach. "I've told you that millions of times."

Wild Thing noticed too.

"I don't know why everyone's making a fuss of Dad," she said loudly. "He's not nearly as interesting as me!"

Typical Wild Thing. But the sun was too warm, and I was having too good a time, to get into an argument with my sister.

While Dad and Harris were buying us drinks, Zach nudged my arm. "Hey – what's everybody so excited about?"

Bonnie and I looked where he was pointing and saw that a small crowd had gathered. We drifted over to see what was going on, and found everyone was waiting to speak with two girls who were signing autographs. They were wearing cowboy boots and print dresses, and one of them was holding a guitar. "I don't recognize them," said Zach.

"They look a bit familiar," I began, and then I noticed two people in the crowd that I definitely *did* recognize. "Uh-oh," I said. "Look who it is."

It was Fiona and Nerisa. They were both wearing T-shirts with *Giddy Girls* printed on them in swirly letters, and Fiona had a mobile phone, which she was using to snap photos whenever the two signing the autographs looked her way.

"Let's make a run for it," Bonnie suggested, "before they see us." But it was too late. They already had.

"I suppose *you* want an autograph too," said Fiona. "You'll just have to wait your turn. *We've* been waiting ages."

We moved closer. "Whose autographs are you waiting for?" I asked.

"Do you mean you don't know?" Fiona stared at me as if she couldn't believe her ears. "I'd have thought even *you* would have heard of the Giddy Girls, Kate." From the way she spoke, you'd think I'd said I hadn't heard of the Queen.

"Well, I haven't," I snapped. Actually, this wasn't true. Now I came to think of it, I *had* heard of them. Simone and Lucille – the Giddy Girls. I'd listened to a couple of their songs. And my friend Tabitha had a big poster of them on her bedroom wall. They were a new girl band, and a lot of people at school were really into them.

"We're their biggest fans," Fiona announced. "We're going to get our photos taken with them, aren't we, Nerisa? Maybe you lot could take the photos. I don't expect you've anything else to do."

"I will," said Wild Thing at once. (I decided not to tell Fiona that Wild Thing's speciality is taking photos with her thumb in them.)

While we'd been talking, the queue for autographs had been dwindling.

"So do you want that signed?" one of the

Giddy Girls asked Fiona, who was holding an autograph book. Then she leaned over and looked straight at me. "Hey, I love your stripe!"

I blushed. I'd forgotten about my purple stripe.

"I did it!" said Wild Thing at once.

"Funky! Did you really?"

"I helped," said Bonnie quickly.

Simone was looking at Wild Thing, who was miming being a hairdresser: *snip, snip snip*. "Wow, kid, I'll be coming to you for my next hair appointment."

"OK," said Wild Thing. "If I've got time."

Simone laughed. Fiona was looking like she was about to explode. "I know all of your songs," she told Simone, and she tried to elbow Wild Thing out of the way. "Listen. *Giddy girl, in a whirl*—" and she started singing the chorus to their latest hit.

Bonnie said loudly to Simone, "We're in a band, you know. Kate's dad is in a band too. They're playing this afternoon."

"That so?" Lucille had come over to join us.

She had a guitar slung over her back and dramatic red hair.

"Yes, he does play," Wild Thing said. "But he's not very good."

"Wild Thing!"

"Well, he's not good like me on my violin."

I was gasping with horror at this, but Simone and Lucille were laughing. "Is she really called Wild Thing? That's just like the Monkey Magic song—"

"Yes, that's our dad," I said, before Wild Thing could say anything else. "I mean, he wrote that song."

"What!" gasped Lucille.

"No way!" said Simone.

"You mean—" whispered Lucille.

And they both burst out: "Your dad's in Monkey Magic! You're Tom Brent's kids!"

They were both exclaiming, and I suddenly realized that they were just as big fans of Monkey Magic, and our dad's music, as Fiona and Nerisa were of *them*. Lucille started humming bits of Monkey Magic's songs, and Simone was explaining how they were going to cover one of Dad's songs for their next album. Meanwhile, Fiona was just staring, with her mouth hanging open like a goldfish.

It was at that moment Dad wandered over, saying, "Here are your drinks, kids." At first Simone and Lucille were really shy, and actually stammering they were so nervous, but then they were almost falling over themselves to meet him and tell him how excited they were to be at a festival with Monkey Magic, and how much they loved his music.

Lucille turned to Fiona, who was still standing there gawping.

"Hey, kid, is that a phone you've got there? Would you mind taking a photo of us with Tom? It would mean the world to me."

Fiona just nodded, very, very slowly.

Monkey Magic were going to be playing on the main stage, and as we walked towards it later that afternoon, I realized that although I'd heard Dad and Wes play loads of times (usually in our living room) I'd never actually been to a live performance of the band before. The sun was beaming down, and everybody was wearing sunglasses and hats and swigging bottles of water, and everyone was cheerful. It was a really strange feeling, as the crowd grew and grew: every space filling up with people who wanted to watch my dad play.

I had earplugs for Wild Thing and me (Dad had insisted, in case the music got too loud) and he'd also said that we must be sure to stay close to Harris and Gran. So we did. Bonnie and Zach were there too, hopping about with excitement.

When the band came onstage, everyone went crazy. For a moment I just stared around at all the screaming people (well, except Gran, who was shaking her head as if she thought they'd all gone mad). Then the mood of the crowd swept over me, and I started cheering too.

Wes was holding the microphone (he's the lead singer), Mick was on drums, Luke on bass, and Chris and Dad were playing guitar. I thought Dad was looking great. He keeps in good shape – for a dad. And he was wearing his cool jacket and his shades.

They started with their hit song "Fiery Mountain". The rest of the crowd joined in with the chorus (*and we'll watch the lava flow. . .*) and we all joined in too. We really yelled it out. Then came Dad's guitar solo (well, guitar *duo* really, as he and Chris were both playing) and Zach started playing air guitar. Wild Thing played air guitar too.

With every song, the crowd got more and more into the music. They swayed during the slow songs, and they jumped about during the fast ones. For a while Gran just stood there, pursing her lips. But then I looked round and. . .

"Gran! You're dancing!" I yelled. She took no notice – just went right on jumping about with everyone else.

The song ended. Wes spoke into the microphone. "It's great to be here again – at Brammingham Festival," he said. (The crowd cheered as if he had said something amazing. I guess they would have cheered him whatever he said.) "Brammingham was one of the first gigs we ever did. And now we're back again, in our original line-up, with Tom on guitar. And we're going to sing a song I know you all love, just to finish off. . ."

Dad and Chris played a few chords on the guitar. Wild Thing pulled at my sleeve. "It's *my song!*" she squealed, so loudly that I could hear her clearly despite the noise and the earplugs. "It's 'Wild Thing'!"

Wild Thing has always thought that the Monkey Magic song "Wild Thing" is about her – even though Dad says it isn't. And he should know. He wrote it. But that doesn't stop Wild Thing acting like it's her personal property.

"*I'm* singing it!" she shouted.

"OK, then," I said. I reckoned most of the crowd would be singing along anyway.

"I mean from up there," Wild Thing yelled, pointing at the stage. And she set off through the crowd.

"Wild Thing – come back!" I lunged at her, trying to grab the back of her T-shirt, but she was too quick. I could see her just ahead of me, but every time I thought I was close enough to catch her, there was someone in the way.

"Please let me through," I begged, but the crowd were mainly listening to Wes, who was still talking.

". . .some very special people we want to join us. . ."

Suddenly a gap opened up and I made the most of it.

"Stop!"

I leapt forward and grabbed my sister. She didn't like it and began to scream and struggle. But I held on determinedly. I wasn't going to let Wild Thing embarrass us all by climbing onto that stage!

". . .and that's why we'd like Kate and Josephine to come onto the stage now. And their pals Zach and Bonnie, of course." I blinked confusedly. It was Wes speaking. What did he mean, go on to the stage?

"If you could let them get through, guys,"

Wes went on. "And if you're not sure who they are, they're the two girls having the fisticuffs halfway towards the back."

Suddenly everybody was staring at us. It was *so* embarrassing. I let go of Wild Thing quickly, but she hadn't worked out that the fight was over, and whacked me in the stomach.

"Ouch! Stop that," I hissed at her.

And then Zach and Bonnie were there with us, and the crowd was parting to let us through, and everyone clapped as we all walked across the grass (I spotted the Giddy Girls waving, and Fiona and Nerisa with their mouths hanging open) to where Dad and Wes were waiting to pull us on to the stage.

16

The only thing was, when we were standing there, looking out over all those people in the crowd, all of them waiting to hear us play, I suddenly lost my nerve.

"I can't do this," I told Dad. "You know I hate people watching me!"

"Just relax, Kate," said Dad, grinning. "I've got your guitar. You'll be fine."

He produced my guitar from the side of the stage. I did feel better when it was in my hands, but then when I looked at the crowd, I could feel myself panicking again.

"I just don't think—"

"Kate is a scaredy-cat," said Wild Thing in a loud voice.

"I am not!" I snapped. And that was that.

There was no way I was getting down now!

In fact, as soon as the music began again, I started to feel better. Zach had his guitar too, and Bonnie her tambourine (I guess Dad and Susie must have organized it all between them) and then, to my amazement and absolute horror, Dad went to the side of the stage and brought back—

"My violin!" howled Wild Thing in delight.

"Are you mad?" I hissed at Dad, as Wild Thing stuck her violin under her chin, then almost took Bonnie's eye out with her bow.

He winked at me. "Don't worry, Kate."

I'm not sure what the crowd thought as Wild Thing stepped forward for an impromptu violin recital. It can't have been what they were expecting. Or wanting. However, as I guess Dad had known all along, she didn't have a microphone close by, and so they couldn't hear much of her anyway. Wild Thing played a few bars of "Twinkle, Twinkle, Little Star". Then, when she forgot which note came next, we all came crashing in playing "Wild Thing".

She's a demon child
She's not meek and mild
She's wild!
Oh yeah. . .

She can bite
Oh yeah and she can fight!
She'll give you a fright!
Oh yeah!

Luckily Zach and I know this song pretty well. And Bonnie couldn't go far wrong on her tambourine. As for Wild Thing herself, she soon decided to abandon her violin in favour of leaping around the stage with Wes and bawling out the words – which she knows by heart. After all, it's one of her favourite songs.

She's wild, wild, wild!
Yeah!
Oh she's wild, wild, wild. . .

We finished up with a storming crescendo, Wild Thing and Wes both went sliding across the stage, and the crowd went crazy. We all waved and bowed and waved again. And that was the end of our first ever festival gig.

*

That night, we all gathered down by the tents. We had put ours up next to Susie's, at a safe distance from the river. Dad made a real campfire, and we fetched logs from the woods to sit on. Then we roasted sausages on sticks over the flames, just the way Wild Thing had always wanted, and gobbled them up with crusty bread rolls and tomato ketchup and sliced onions. They were delicious – even the burnt bits. The dogs sat and watched every bite, and were in there like a flash if anyone dropped some.

Wes came to join us, and so did Gran. She sat on a deckchair rather than a log, but she didn't tell Dad off about the flood (or not more than ten minutes' worth), and she really enjoyed her sausage.

"What about your friend Julia?" I asked curiously. "Didn't you want to have dinner with her in the camper van?"

Gran coughed. "Well, to be honest with you, Julia is . . . how shall I put this . . ."

I chewed my sausage while she searched for the right word.

". . . sulking."

I almost choked. *"Sulking?"*

I didn't think grandmothers had sulks. They were meant to be too old and wise.

"Yes. She feels that you and Wild Thing have somehow stolen her grandchildren's thunder . . . especially when she heard about your performance onstage."

"Ah," I said.

I knew Fiona and Nerisa had been watching, and they couldn't have liked what they saw. They *definitely* hadn't liked it when the Giddy Girls congratulated us afterwards (lots of other people did too) and insisted on taking our photos and getting our autographs. They said that I had a "quirky charm" and that Wild Thing was "really wild" (well, they weren't wrong there)!

Not only that, they had actually asked us if we'd like to be their backing singers. It turned out they were shooting a video for their new song soon, and they wanted Wild Thing, Bonnie and me to take part!

It was nice to be asked, but Dad had refused to consider it for a moment. He'd said straight out that he didn't approve of "celebrity culture" and he thought "ordinary childhood was important" and "it wasn't right for his kids". He said us appearing on the stage had been a one-off, and it didn't mean we were going to start prancing around on music videos and be splashed all over the internet.

I suppose he has a point. Wild Thing is a big enough show-off as it is – she would go completely crazy if she became a celebrity. As for me – well, since the hair-dye disaster, I kind of felt that Dad was right. I was happy just to be me.

(Still, I *was* secretly pleased that Fiona had heard them ask us. I reckoned she'd be a lot more polite to us from now on.)

I stared across at Wild Thing, who was busy cramming marshmallows on to a stick. She had a big, smoky smudge on her face and ketchup round her mouth, and muddy boots, and muddy clothes, and scratches on her arm and cheeks. She looked up at me and grinned.

"I've put twelve marshmallows on my stick," she announced. "And I'm going to eat them *all*."

Gran heaved a big sigh. "Hopeless!" she muttered.

"Are you really disappointed in us, Gran?" I asked. "I know you'd like us to be more like Fiona and Nerisa."

They wouldn't have been stuffing their faces with twelve marshmallows. *They* wouldn't have been covered top to toe in mud.

But Gran turned and looked at me in astonishment. "What are you talking about?"

"You know you think they're wonderful."

"I don't know what gave you that idea!"

"Well, Mum," Dad said, overhearing, "you have rather acted like the sun shines out of their—"

"Tom!" Gran interrupted. "Anyway, I don't know what you're talking about. I've never thought that much of those girls really." She paused while we stared at her accusingly. "Well, maybe I did think they were well-behaved . . . and polite . . . and neat and tidy too . . . but when I heard them whinging and whining in the camper van just now, all because Kate and Josephine had impressed those Giddy-up Girls—"

"*Giddy* Girls. Not Giddy-up."

Gran waved a hand dismissively. "They're both silly names. Anyway, when I heard them being such moaning minnies, I found I'd changed my mind."

I squeezed Gran's hand.

"You didn't really think I could prefer them to you and Josephine, did you?" Gran shook her head. "Really, Kate, you are a silly billy sometimes. I love you more than I can say, and I even love Wild Thing – the grubby little mud-covered monster!"

I gave Gran a hug. Then I grinned at Dad, and at Wild Thing, whose cheeks were bulging like a hamster's. I felt like everything was just about as good as it could be.

The adults started chatting among themselves. "I reckon this has been the best camping trip ever," I said to Bonnie, who was putting pinecones onto the fire.

Wild Thing overheard me.

"No, it hasn't. We haven't met a bear."

"There aren't any bears, Wild Thing, we keep telling you!"

It was getting dark. Outside the flickering firelight of our campfire, the shadows were thick and black. There were rustlings in the undergrowth. And as I stared at the woods around, I thought it was the kind of night when you could almost – almost – believe you might meet a bear.

And *that's* when we heard it. A low snarling from the undergrowth.

The adults were still chatting. "Dad!" I hissed. Then I turned and stared hard at the patch where the snarling had come from.

"It must have been the dogs," whispered Bonnie. But she didn't sound certain.

"No, the dogs are all begging for sausages."

Bonnie and I looked at each other. Neither of us wanted to admit it, but we were scared.

Wild Thing got to her feet. *She* wasn't worried. She called out, "Here, bear! Come and get some marshmallows!" then set off into the shadows.

"Wild Thing, come back!"

A dark shape lumbered out of the undergrowth. The dogs forgot about the sausages. They looked at the shape, and whined.

"There *is* a bear!" shouted Wild Thing. "Look, I can see it moving!"

Then everything happened very quickly. Dad realized what was going on and leapt to pull Wild Thing back from danger. I went running in too. Before we could reach her, with a terrific snarl, the beast sprang. Wild Thing screamed at the top of her lungs. . .

Hound Dog, Sugar and Sweet rushed forward. The next moment, the dogs were all charging around in the undergrowth, playing tug with two furry brown picnic rugs, while Harris and

Zach, who had been hiding under the rugs, were rolling around in the mud yelling with laughter.

"It was my idea!" yelled Wild Thing delightedly. "Did you believe it was a bear? Did you, Kate?"

"No!" I told her. "Nobody did!"

"Not true!" said Wild Thing gleefully. She was right!

It took a while for my heart to stop pounding. I wasn't about to admit it, but they had taken me in hook, line and sinker.

Everyone around us was laughing and roasting marshmallows.

"One day I'll find a real bear," Wild Thing told me.

"Maybe you will," I said. After all, my little sister doesn't give up easily. If there was a bear to be found . . . well then, I reckoned she would find it.

But for the moment there was just one crazy creature in the woods. And their name was:

WILD THING!

Emma Barnes has always been a
bookworm. She was born and raised in Edinburgh,
where she spent hours making up stories for
her younger sister. Emma's first writing success
came when she won a short-story competition –
the prize was a pair of shoes. Emma wears the
shoes for school visits, where she loves to spark
children's imaginations and create a passion for
writing and stories. Emma now lives in Yorkshire
with her husband, daughter and Rocky the dog.

www.emmabarnes.info